Love Found in Sherwood Forest

Linda Shenton Matchett

Love Found in Sherwood Forest
By Linda Shenton Matchett

Cover Design and author photo by: Wes Matchett

PHOTO CREDITS: Serhii Chernetskyi from Pixabay

ISBN-13: 978-0-9985265-0-8

To Wes For Everything

Chapter One

With a Tony award-winning performance, Leighanne Webster pretended to listen to her sister's prattle during the ride from England's Manchester airport. She smiled and occasionally murmured noncommittal sounds when Kelli glanced at her from the driver's seat. Leighanne peeked at her watch and silently calculated the number of hours she had been awake. Too many.

Kelli's voice broke in. "What do you think, sis?"

Leighanne searched her memory. What had they been talking about? "Whatever you want is fine with me."

"You're sure you don't mind going to the castle before dropping off your bags at the flat?"

Kelli hadn't noticed her lack of attention. What a relief! No need to hurt her sister's feelings, especially since she had unwittingly thrown her a lifeline with the invitation to come to England. "I don't mind. I'm anxious to see the place." She tossed Kelli a wry grin. "I haven't been in a castle since leaving Britain. We don't have any in New York City, you know."

"You used to. During the 1920s, a couple of the Vanderbilt

mansions came close, from what I understand. Too bad they were demolished."

"Only you would think of that. You should have been a history teacher."

Kelli shook her head. "I'm happier being a docent. The people who come to the museum actually want to be there, unlike a classroom full of kids waiting for the bell to ring. Nottingham Castle is beautiful, but wait till you see Newstead Abbey and Wollaton Hall. They're magnificent."

Leighanne nodded and looked out the side window. The past melded with the present: a tudor-style bungalow stood shoulder to shoulder with a glass and brick sky scraper, a stone cottage huddled next to a terraced brownstone. Shops with clever names like The Worm That Turned and Windblowers dotted the storefronts.

The angry gray clouds that followed them from the airport finally opened and poured out their contents. Kelli turned on the wipers, and they fought to clear the deluge from the windshield. Leighanne pulled her coat closed and tucked her scarf around her neck. "Must be summer in England; it's raining."

"Cute, sis. I suppose it was sunny and warm in New York when you left."

"And humid. A balmy eighty-six degrees."

Shuddering, Kelli said, "Ugh. I'll take cold and rainy over hot and humid any day."

"That's why you're still in England, and I'm not."

A smile split Kelli's face. "No, you left because you wanted to become a Broadway star. And you've done it. Tell me again why you're willing to leave all that behind to help little-old-me produce the annual play for the Robin Hood Pageant."

Despite the chill in the car, sweat sprang out on Leighanne's forehead. She pasted on a smile and said, "Uh, a break. I just needed a break between productions. Your request came at the perfect time." The lie slid out easily.

Kelli took her hand off the steering wheel to reach over and give Leighanne's hand a quick pat. "I'm glad. It's been too long since the Webster sisters have spent time together."

Leighanne released her pent up breath. "Can we play tourist for a bit? I'll bet Nottingham has some great sightseeing. I never got here when we lived in London. I need to visit Sherwood Forest; wouldn't you say? Get a look at Major Oak and other places associated with the legend. Better to help you."

"There will be plenty of time for that, and there's lots to look at: Green's Windmill, Market Square, the Arts Centre, sculptures and statues. You're going to love it."

Leighanne settled back against the seat. Maybe this trip wasn't a bad idea after all. No one knew where she was. She didn't have the stress of auditioning. No deadlines. The tightness in her chest eased. Yes, this trip was just what the doctor ordered.

Kelli navigated the car through the narrow streets. The rain had slowed to a steady drizzle. A sandstone-colored wall appeared to their left, and she followed it to an open iron gate where she turned into the parking lot. The vehicle bumped and shimmied over the cobblestones then glided onto the asphalt lane past pristine formal gardens filled with a rainbow of blossoms. Amid the trees on the promontory perched a multi-turreted, colored castle.

After Kelli pulled to a stop in front of the entrance, the women stepped out of the car and hurried through the mist into the castle. Their heels clattered on the floor, the sound echoing throughout the stone and brick entryway. A thirty-foot ceiling hovered above their heads, and the walls held a collection of oil paintings and needlepoint banners. Dampness filled the air.

Kelli and Leighanne slid out of their wet coats and hung them with several others on a freestanding rack. A faded brown rug caught the water as it dripped to the floor. Leighanne stopped in front of a small mirror and gave her frizzy hair a critical frown. Why couldn't she have her sister's silky blonde hair inherited from their father? No, she had to have her mother's mass of unkempt, brillo-pad hair. She pushed the loose strands back from her face, but they sprang back into position. Rolling her eyes, she turned to follow her sister who was disappearing through a door at the end of the massive foyer.

Leighanne trotted after her sister then froze when the throng of cast members on the temporary wooden platform turned as one to stare at her. She forced herself to breathe as she raised a hand in greeting.

The group applauded, and heat suffused her face. So much for anonymity. When the clapping ceased, Kelli said, "As you can see, we're excited you're here to help us out. You can meet everyone as we go along. I've made them promise they'll treat you like one of the crowd." She looked at her watch. "The director should be here shortly."

Forcing herself forward, Leighanne nodded. "Nice to see you all. We're going to have a lot of fun together. Is there an extra copy of the script? I--"

Heavy footsteps sounded behind her. She pivoted and nearly stumbled as a chill swept over her. Walking toward her with a broad grin on his face was Jamison Blake, her ex-fiancé.

"Hello, Leighanne. Good to see you again."

Chapter Two

Jamison watched as emotions played over Leighanne's face, the first of which was shock. Apparently, Kelli had failed to mention his part in the production to her sister. He'd like to be a fly on the wall during that conversation when it happened. He had been surprised when Kelli told him Leighanne had agreed to help out. Now, he knew why. She had no idea he'd be involved.

His gaze flicked over her. She was beautiful, albeit a bit fatigued from the long travel day. Leave it to Kelli to bring her here straight from the airport. Leighanne was either too gracious or too tired to say no. A tangle of dark curls framed her wan face, and gray smudges lay under her red-rimmed eyes. Although rumpled, her teal pant suit and matching shoes looked expensive. Stunning, no matter how long the trip.

He tossed a glance at Kelli. "Sorry, I'm late. We had a last minute tour which took longer than expected."

"No problem. We've only been here a few moments."

Leighanne was mute, but her glare was unmistakable. She was

not happy to see him. He started to move past her, and she came alive. Her hands closed into tight fists. She spoke through thin lips, "Late? What do you mean *late*? What are you doing here? Surely, you're not part of this."

He held his hands up in surrender. "I'm afraid so. I'm the director."

Her eyes widened. "The director? You can't be. Kelli would have told me." She whirled toward her sister who gave a sheepish shrug.

Leighanne hissed, "Are you kidding me? *He's* the director, and you didn't think to tell me?" Realization dawned. "Wait a minute. You didn't tell me on purpose. You knew I wouldn't come." She whirled back to Jamison. "Well, I can leave just as easily as I arrived."

She stalked past him and out the door leaving a wake of familiar floral scent. He closed his eyes for a moment against the memories that washed over him. The cast began to whisper. Squaring his shoulders, he approached the stage and beckoned to Kelli. She followed him off-stage where they could speak in private.

He leaned close, so she could hear him. "Did you really think she'd stay once she found out I was here? She's never forgiven me."

"You need to give her time."

"Give her time? It's been five years."

Kelli grimaced. "She does have a long memory. I'm sure she still holds grudges for things I did to her in the crib."

He gave her a crooked grin. "Surely, she's not that bad."

"You tell me. You saw her reaction."

"I know, but I *had* to break the engagement. It was for her own good. She never would have accepted that first play on Broadway, and she would have resented me. It's better this way. She's the accomplished actress she should be."

"Happiness isn't about success, Jamison. Besides, Leighanne may be a star, but she isn't happy. She hasn't told me what's going on, and she's making a valiant effort to appear like she has it all together, but something's wrong. And this play is just the thing to take her mind off whatever it is."

"If you say so. Maybe you should find another director."

Kelli reared back. "Absolutely not! You've been preparing this for months. Besides it's too late. Who would we get to take your place?"

He pointed at her. "You. And Leighanne can handle the producing on her own."

Shaking her head, she patted his arm. "You're not getting out of this, no matter how hard you try. Besides, I need you to be my prayer partner. That's what Leighanne really needs. She's hurting, and God is the only one who can heal her. Are you with me?"

Jamison hesitated. Kelli was right. God was the answer for Leighanne, even though she didn't know it or probably want it. He turned away and sent a prayer skyward. *Is this your plan for me, Lord? To be part of Leighanne's life again? I don't know if I can be just friends, even if she'll accept me. I still love her, Father. I realized that the moment I saw her.*

I love her too, my son. She needs me. Help her return to me.

Peace flooded him. He would stay. It might be the hardest thing he would ever do. That was an understatement, but he would be obedient. Turning back to Kelli, he held out his hand. "Partners, it is."

Kelli beamed at him, and they shook hands.

"Kelli!"

Prop master Tom Haddonfield trotted toward them, concern etched on his face. He cradled a quiver of arrows in his arms. He pulled several arrows from inside and held them out. The shafts had been snapped in half and the fletchings torn off. "Most of the arrows are missing, and the remaining ones are like this."

Kelli put her hand to her throat. "How is that possible? There are over five hundred arrows."

Tom shook his head. "I don't know, but every single one is broken."

"What are we going to do? The lead-time on them is weeks.

We could order more, but they would never arrive in time."

Jamison plucked one from Tom's grasp and studied it. "We could work extra hours and make them ourselves."

Kelli and Tom looked skeptical, and Jamison said, "What choice do we have? We can't exactly do the fight scene without weapons."

Kelli took the arrow from him. "We could cut that scene out of the play."

Jamison scowled. "No, that's the climax of the production. Whoever did this wants us to fail, and I won't let that happen. Even if I have to work twenty-four hours a day from now until the first performance."

Tom dumped the broken shafts back into the quiver. "You won't have to do that. I'm sure the cast members would help."

Jamison shook his head. "We have to keep this among ourselves as best we can. It might be one of them who did this."

Kelli's brow furrowed. "You think so? Why?"

"I don't know, but until we find out differently, I think we should act like nothing has happened."

"How will we get the arrows made in time?"

Jamison gestured to Tom. "Leave that to us." He gave Kelli a one-armed hug. "And add it to the prayer list. Now, how about you tell the cast to get into their places for the beginning of the second act. I'll be there in a minute."

"Okay." She gave the two of them a long look before approaching the stage.

Jamison turned back to Tom. "Now, about these arrows."

Tom put a finger to his lips for a second. "Before we talk about that, there's something else. I didn't want to say anything to Kelli. She'd shut the play down for sure."

Jamison raised an eyebrow and waited while Tom dug a scrap of paper from the back pocket of his pants. He unfolded it and held it out. In large font it said:

CAST LEIGHANNE WEBSTER AS MARIAN OR IT WILL BE WORSE NEXT TIME.

Chapter Three

Leighanne descended the stairs, her slippered feet whispering against the wooden treads. She crossed the living room and entered the dining room where Kelli and her husband Maurice sat with their twins, Charlotte and Edmund.

The children scrambled from their chairs and grabbed her in a group hug. Leighanne met her sister's eyes above the kids' heads and offered her a tentative smile, an olive branch after the afternoon tantrum. The siblings' chatter made talking unnecessary. Kelli's smile was remote, and Leighanne gave an inward sigh. She had once again damaged their tenuous relationship. Maybe she should leave. They were a better long-distance family.

She tousled the children's hair and nudged them toward their seats before sliding into one of the empty places on the other side of the table. Maurice reached for her plate and began to fill it from the various platters of food. He looked over the glasses perched on his nose at the youngsters and said, "Give your aunt a chance to get settled. You'll have plenty of time to badger her during her visit."

His piercing eyes nailed her to the chair. "You *will* be staying, won't you?"

Shooting a glance at her sister's downcast face, she spoke in a low voice, "That remains to be seen."

Maurice raised an eyebrow and frowned, spearing his carrots in a stiff motion. He would take her sister's side; of that there was no doubt. "We'll discuss this after the meal, when the children have been dismissed."

Leighanne nodded, caught between anger and remorse. She lifted a forkful of fluffy mashed potatoes, their herbal aroma wafting toward her. Cooking: another one of Kelli's gifts. She, on the other hand, knew how to order take-out. The potatoes melted in her mouth, and she moaned. "Kelli, these are delicious. It's amazing what you can do with a simple root vegetable."

Her sister spoke through tight lips, "Thank you. I know they're one of your favorites and would imagine you don't get a chance to eat at home very often."

Charlotte barged into the conversation waving her spoon as she talked. "Aunt Leighanne, Mummy says we can take some time off from school to visit the sights with you. Isn't that great? I can't wait to show you everything. You'll have to see Nottingham Castle, but we have better ones than that. And we have to go to Sherwood Forest. You can't do a play about Robin Hood without seeing that, don't you think? And the caves, too! We have to go to the caves."

Maurice laid his hand on Charlotte's arm. "That doesn't mean you can skip out on your studies. You'll have to work extra hard in the evenings."

Charlotte shrugged. "That's okay. I've already been working ahead. I told Miss Siegel about it weeks ago, and she agreed to help me. What about you, Edmund?"

He finished chugging his milk, set down the glass with a thunk, then wiped the white liquid mustache from his upper lip. "I'm working on it. I still have a book report to write and some extra math problems to do." He looked at Kelli. "Mother, can we go tomorrow? I have a spelling test, and I need more time to get ready."

Kelli centered her fork on the plate and wiped her mouth with the ivory linen napkin. "I'm afraid not, Edmund. There was damage to some of the props, and we need to fix them tomorrow. Maybe Aunt Leighanne can help you prepare for your test. English was one of her best subjects. And she won the spelling bee three years in a row."

"Is that true, Aunt Leighanne? Three years in a row! You must be really smart."

Leighanne flushed as she nodded. "Just a good speller, Edmund. I'd be happy to help you after your mom and I talk about the play for a bit. How's that sound?"

Edmund grinned and pointed at her with his fork. "Sounds like you want to get rid of us kids. We always miss the good stuff."

Leighanne returned his smile as Kelli broke in, "Edmund, don't wave your utensils. And you'll get to hear the *good stuff* soon enough. Now, if you're finished eating, go work on your spelling words. Aunt Leighanne will be up soon. Charlotte, you too."

The pair slid off their chairs and left the room. Maurice raised his voice, "And no listening from the stairs!"

Their giggles faded as they bounded to the second floor. Maurice slid his empty plate toward the middle of the table and swallowed the last of his water. He pushed back his chair and stood. "I've mediated your arguments in the past, but I think I'll leave you to it tonight. It's time you learned to work out your differences."

Kelli folded her arms across her chest. "We don't need your help."

He leaned down and kissed the top of her head. "I know." Wagging his finger at the two of them, he continued, "Don't come out until you've made up."

His footsteps receded, and an awkward silence settled on the room.

"Leighanne--"

"Listen--"

Kelli clamped her lips together, and Leighanne gestured to her. "You first."

"No, you go ahead."

Leighanne sat back, shaking her head. "I insist you have your say." She made a zipping motion across her mouth. "And I promise to be quiet until you're finished."

"All right. I just want to say I'm sorry I didn't tell you about Jamison. It was selfish of me, I know. I guess I didn't realize how much the break up still hurt you. We need your help, and I couldn't think of anyone else I could count on. He offered to quit after you left today, but I told him no, that we'd figure out a way to make it work." She raised her eyes to Leighanne's. "Please say you'll stay."

Leighanne blew out a breath. How could she say no to her sister? Yet, how could she look at Jamison every day knowing he had rejected her...that somehow she was unworthy of his love? He had seen some flaw in her he couldn't live with. She had to choose between her sister and her pride.

"You don't understand--"

Kelli leaned forward. "Then help me. Tell me what's bothering you, what brought you to England...or at least what chased you out of the States."

Leighanne searched Kelli's face. They used to share secrets. When had that changed? When had everything become a competition? "I still can't believe you didn't tell me about Jamison. That was low."

"I've already apologized. I need your help. It galls me to have to ask for it, and now you're making me beg. If I had another option, I would have taken it. I know you won't believe it, but you are a much needed answer to prayer."

Leighanne slumped back in the chair. "Now you're going to pull the God-card?"

A frown darkened Kelli's face. "Fine. We won't talk about God or Jamison. Can we talk about how to make it work for you to stay?"

Leighanne shoved her chair back then got up and began to pace. She stopped in front of Kelli, arms wrapped around her middle. "All right! I'll tell you. I was fired. That's why I have time to help you. There. I've said it. Are you happy now? Maybe I'm not such a great actress after all."

Kelli's mouth gaped. She made a move to get up, and Leighanne held up a hand. "Don't you dare try to hug me."

"You don't always have to be the strong one, you know. It's okay to be upset." She ran her finger along a flower pattern in the tablecloth before raising her eyes to Leighanne. "This could be a chance for you to imagine your life as something else: an actress on the London stage or maybe a director or producer? How about film? Just because one director didn't like your work, doesn't mean you're not a great actress. Our little play could be just the thing to get your mind off the situation in New York, help your pride heal."

"My pride!"

"Sure, that's what's wounded. Otherwise, you wouldn't be so angry."

Leighanne flopped back into the chair. At least Kelli hadn't asked why she had been let go.

Heavy footsteps clattered down the stairs. The women toward the doorway, and Maurice appeared with the cordless phone in his hand. He held it out to Kelli. "It's Jamison. Louise Durand has broken her leg."

Kelli blanched. "Oh, no!"

Leighanne's gaze ricocheted between Kelli and Maurice. "What? Who is Louise?"

Kelli turned panic-filled eyes to her. "Maid Marian. She's the woman who's playing Maid Marian."

Chapter Four

Leighanne sat behind the crowd of cast members with her back propped against the cold, stone wall. She chewed her lower lip while Kelli stood in front of the group, a clipboard clenched in one hand and the other periodically rubbing her wrinkled forehead. Jamison perched on a stool to Kelli's right. Leighanne forced herself to focus on her sister rather than his angular frame. She caught him staring at her when she sat down.

Kelli cleared her throat, and a hush fell over the troupe. "Okay, folks, listen up. I've got some bad news, and I only want to say it once. Louise Durand is in the hospital with a broken leg." The company rustled, and she raised her voice over the noise, "Quiet, please. Quiet!" She paused until silence descended. "Thanks. She's in surgery right now, so when I'm finished with my announcement, I'd like us to have a time of prayer for her. As you know, there are five weeks until the performance—plenty of time for someone to step in and memorize the lines. Leighanne has kindly agreed to take the role temporarily, until we find a replacement."

Several of the cast members turned toward Leighanne and applauded. She flushed as the clapping spread through the group. Glowing faces smiled at her. Moisture slicked her palms, and her heart raced. Her breathing came in gasps. How would she ever pull this off? The thought of reading from the script sent her into a tailspin. She should never have come. Surely in a city the size of Nottingham, there were plenty of people who could do the part. What was she thinking when she said yes? It seemed like a good idea at the time. She wanted to patch things up with Kelli, and it seemed like the right way to do it. Until now. Now it was stupidity, plain and simple. She raised a hand to acknowledge the cheering, her lips curved in a stiff smile.

Kelli continued, "If any of you know of someone who might be a good fit, have them contact me for an audition."

A voice spoke from within the group, "We have someone. Leighanne would be perfect." A hum of conversation started.

Kelli rescued her. "No, we need to find a community member. Leighanne is here to help me as producer and only agreed to run lines as a favor to me. Remember, she's on a break from acting. We need to honor that. Meanwhile, I'll review the list of folks who auditioned and didn't get selected to see if one of them might work out. Any questions?"

Leighanne studied the floor aware of the glances from the

others. Aware of their judgment. Aware that once again she was letting someone down. Movement from the side caused her to look up. Jamison's gaze rested on her, and she gulped before looking away. Was that disappointment on his face? Pity? Did it matter what he thought?

Finger combing her hair, she closed her eyes. Yes, it mattered. It mattered a lot.

Kelli's voice broke through her thoughts and scattered them like leaves on a windy day. "I'll say a prayer for Louise then we'll start rehearsing the last scene."

Leighanne studied her hands as her sister prayed, "Father, we lift Louise up to you tonight. Guide the surgeon's hands as they operate on her. Heal her quickly and with minimal pain. Wrap her in your arms and keep her safe. Thank you for caring for her, for each one of us. We love you and thank you. In Your Son's name, amen."

The actors stood and dispersed in clumps, a cacophony of voices filling the air. Leighanne made her way to the stage, script clutched in one hand. She licked her dry lips and took a deep breath. Ahead of her, Robin Hood and Little John trotted up the stairs and onto the platform. She gripped the railing and trudged up behind them.

Jamison clapped his hands to get their attention, and the trio turned toward him. He pointed to the far corner. "Little John, you stand back there and pretend you've just dropped out of a tree." He swept his arm to the opposite side of the set. "Maid Marian, you and Robin are standing over there. We'll begin with John's line 'Robin, I have news!' Everyone, ready?"

Leighanne's pulse thrummed in her ears. Could they hear that? She flipped through the script, her vision blurring the print. Where is that line? Why can't I see? Is it warm in here? Pinpricks of light sparkled in front of her, and her breathing came in short gasps. Her head swam. She swayed. Jamison's voice rumbled, the words indistinct. Light-headed, she reached for something to hold her up. Her fingers swiped at empty air, and she crumpled to the floor. Then all was black.

———————◆———————

Leighanne's eyelids fluttered against the light. She was laying on something soft. What happened? The memory of her last moments of consciousness flooded into her head, and she flushed. She had fainted. More specifically, she had had a panic attack then fainted. Now they would all know why she was "in between productions." Why she had been fired. And they wouldn't want her either.

She opened her eyes to find Jamison's face inches from hers. It was filled with concern. Kelli was on her knees nearby, and the cast stood close behind the pair. Leighanne realized she was propped against Jamison's chest with his arm around her shoulder, and she struggled to break free. "I'm fine. I just need some air."

"Lie still. You're not fine. You fainted."

Pushing away from him, she lifted herself to her feet. Her vision tunneled then cleared. "It was the heat. It's way too hot in here."

Jamison rose and turned to the group. "The rest of rehearsal is canceled. Go home and work on your lines. We'll pick up on Thursday."

The crowd moved away and conversation hummed around them. Leighanne scowled. "There is no reason to cancel tonight's practice. I'm fine."

"Maybe if you say that often enough, you'll begin to believe it."

Leighanne glowered at him. Kelli moved toward her, and Leighanne held up a hand. "Stay away. It's bad enough this happened; I don't need you to coddle me."

"We're not coddling you, Leighanne." Jamison spoke with quiet conviction. "We're supporting you. There's a big difference. It's what friends do for one another. You've had a panic attack. It's okay. We'll help you through this."

Leighanne's mouth worked soundlessly as her scowl darted back and forth between Jamison and Kelli. She finally spit out,

"You know about the attacks? How could you?"

Jamison shrugged, a sheepish look on his face. "The wonders of the internet. I've followed your career since you left England. I've read everything ever written about you." He hesitated. "The good and the bad. I saw the articles about the attack that happened during a performance. We thought asking you to come over to help would give you the change you needed to heal."

"Help me heal? This is your way of helping me? Shoving me back into a role? You see how well that worked."

Kelli said, "We didn't think--"

Leighanne exploded. "That's right. You didn't think. Think about this. I will help you produce since that was the original agreement, but you need to find someone else to read for Marian. I will not get back on stage. Not for you. Not for anyone. And when this is over, I'm out of here. Is that clear?"

Chapter Five

The following morning Jamison walked trance-like through Nottingham castle. His mind raced as he parroted the spiel he had given hundreds of times in the past. He could recite it in his sleep. The tour group of rich, white-haired Americans didn't seem to notice his lethargy.

Lord, Kelli and I thought we were doing the right thing. How could we have messed up so badly? Leighanne is going to leave, and I'm never going to see her again. Is that your will?

His heart clenched at the thought of losing Leighanne again. Who was he kidding? To lose her he had to have her, and she made her feelings clear at rehearsal.

The group arrived at the Long Gallery, and he picked up the narrative thread. "For centuries the castle served as one of the most important in England for nobles and royalty alike. Due to its nearness to a crossing of the River Trent, it was in a strategic location. It was also a place of leisure because it was close to the royal hunting grounds in Tideswell as well as the royal forests of

Barnsdale and Sherwood.

"Some have said the castle was occupied by the Sheriff of Nottingham while Richard the Lionheart was away on the Third Crusade. In the legends of Robin Hood, Nottingham Castle is the scene of the final showdown between the Sheriff and the hero outlaw."

A woman near the back of the crowd raised her hand. "Isn't there some sort of production about Robin Hood coming soon?"

He nodded. "Yes, ma'am. In a little over a month, a local community group is producing a play based on one of the more common Robin Hood legends. It will be held at Sunderland Castle."

"Is it true that Broadway star Leighanne Webster is in it?"

"She's helping her sister with production. She's...uh...on a break from acting for the moment. But she has been a tremendous asset."

A snowy-haired woman bent over a walker piped up, "I read she had a nervous breakdown. Do you know anything about that?"

A glimpse of a life under the microscope of public scrutiny shot into Jamison's mind. Poor Leighanne. She didn't even have the luxury of anonymity here in England. Her every move was inspected and dissected by people who knew nothing about her. No wonder she wore a virtual suit of armor around herself. And he and Kelli had yanked off the armor when they pushed her into role-playing. They were no better than the general public.

"Young man?"

"Yes?"

"I asked if you knew anything about Ms. Webster's breakdown?"

He suppressed a scowl, instead putting what he hoped was a noncommittal expression on his face. "I'm afraid not." He gestured toward the paintings. "We'll take about thirty minutes in here so that you can enjoy fine art from Britain and continental Europe. There are works by Nottingham artists such as Thomas Barber, Paul Sandby and others, as well as 20th century works by Ivon Hitchens and Dame Laura Knights. I'll wait here should you have any questions."

Conversation swelled through the room as the tourists drifted toward the paintings. They "oohed" and "aahed" at the masterpieces nestled in heavy wooden frames. Unable to draw a straight line with a ruler, Jamison never tired of this section of the tour—the opportunity to look at beautiful works by men and women to whom God had given the gift of art. Had they taken their talent for granted? Had they known the ability to create came from the great Creator himself?

The woman with the walker caught his eye from across the

room and smiled. He ambled toward her and glanced at the nametag dangling from a lanyard around her neck. "Enjoying yourself, Mrs. Boyer? Are you getting tired? Would you like to sit down?"

Her reedy voice crackled, "I may be old, but I'm not dead yet."

"I meant--"

She poked him with a bony elbow. "I'm teasing you. You're a polite young man. I like that. This seems to be more than a job for you."

"History is my passion. I love it here and often wonder what it would have been like to live eight hundred years ago. I've read books and studied so I know in my head what it was like, but it's hard to understand—especially compared to today's technology. People in the early days of this castle had to dig and scrape out their existence. Nothing was easy." He flushed. "I'm sorry. That's probably more information than you wanted."

She patted his arm. "Not at all." She peered up at him. "Are you married?"

His eyes widened. "I beg your pardon?"

"Are you married? Do you have a wife?"

Leighanne's face filled his mind, and he grimaced. "No, ma'am. I'm single."

"That's too bad. You should find a nice girl and get married. I was married for sixty-four years before my Harold went on to be with the Lord. Sixty-four wonderful years – not always easy, but joyous nonetheless." She winked at him. "I was a child bride, to be sure."

His spirits lifted, and he smiled. "I don't doubt it. You don't look a day over seventy."

She cackled a laugh and jabbed him with her elbow again. He was going to have a bruise for sure. She finished laughing. "Have you been to Ireland and kissed the Blarney stone?"

"No, ma'am."

"Ah, a natural charmer. It's a wonder you haven't already wooed some young woman off her feet."

Jamison shook his finger at her in mock sternness. "When did this become about my love life instead of our gorgeous artwork? We have some breathtaking pieces. You won't want to miss them."

"Changing the subject, are you?"

"Yes!"

"My Harold always said I was a bit of a meddler. How about if you tell me about some of these paintings, and I promise I won't say another word about love."

"You've got yourself a deal."

Jamison sauntered along beside her, the wheels of Mrs. Boyer's walker occasionally squeaking against the polished wood floor.

Jamison regaled her with little known facts about each of the artists. He spied Charles Tillinghast at the end of the room. The play's sponsor wore a frown and leaned against the wall with arms crossed.

What had caused his bad mood?

"Mr. Blake, I would speak with you, please."

"Yes, sir." He turned to Mrs. Boyer. "Will you excuse me for a moment?"

She nodded. "I will take you up on that offer of a seat now."

Jamison guided her to a padded bench a short distance away. He held the walker steady while she lowered herself onto the seat then made his way back to Tillinghast. "What can I do for you, sir?"

"Sucking up to the old ladies, Blake? Smart move. Might translate into something for you."

"I don't know what you mean."

"Most of these old ladies are lonely. Their husbands are dead, and they've got buckets of cash, which won't keep them warm at night. If you play your cards right, maybe one of them will adopt you."

Jamison stiffened and jammed his hands into his pockets where Tillinghast wouldn't see them clenched into fists. Punching the man wouldn't do anyone any good. He hadn't realized until recently how smarmy the guy was, but Jamison would ignore his barbs for now. "What can I do for you, sir?"

Tillinghast stared at him for a long moment. "You can make that Broadway babe of yours get a grip on herself and take the part of Maid Marian permanently. These high-strung actors are trouble, every one of them. But it could mean big money for us, having her name on the marquee."

Bile rose in Jamison's throat. "The original agreement with Ms. Webster was as co-producer with her sister, and we need to honor that."

Poking his finger at Jamison's chest, Tillinghast snarled, "Agreements can be altered. You need to help her change her mind. Producer is one thing, but having her front and center on the stage is what we need. And you're just the man to make it happen. You two used to be engaged, didn't you? Certainly you have some pull with her."

"I doubt that very much."

Tillinghast leaned close and lowered his voice, his dark, pebble-like eyes boring into Jamison's. "You still have all those medical bills associated with your sister's illness, Blake? It would be tough to make those payments without a job. I suggest you do what you're told. It will be good for everyone involved. Who knows—you might even get a promotion out of this! Or maybe those invoices could disappear."

Chapter Six

Leighanne gripped the paintbrush tighter and dipped it into the can near her ankle. She swabbed the brush against the lip of the container then lifted it to the wooden tree that reached toward the ceiling. In one smooth motion, she covered the plywood with rich brown latex. To her right, Kelli and two of the stage crew worked on identical trees. Tom Haddonfield was hunched over a pile of dowels in an effort to replace the broken arrows.

For several minutes, she lost herself in the monotony of the job. Bend. Dip. Swab. Lift. Paint. Repeat.

No one blabbing at her. No one pressing her to do a favor. Her eyes slid away from the tree to the woman working next to her. What was her name? Darlene? Donna? Deborah! That was it.

As if she heard her name, the woman looked over and smiled. "Thanks for helping us out." Her voice was husky and warm.

"My pleasure." Where had that come from? Was it a pleasure? She had to admit she was enjoying being out of the spotlight—just one of the gang. Even after her panic attack, the troupe had treated her with the same friendly acceptance they had when she arrived. So different than New York where everyone had an agenda.

Deborah dabbed paint on her tree. "What do you like to do in your spare time? That is, if you ever get any."

Leighanne hesitated, and the woman rushed on. "I don't mean to pry. I thought it might be nice for you to talk about something other than acting. I cross-stitch. Do you have any hobbies?"

"You're not prying. I don't get a lot of down time, but when I do, I like to knit."

"Really? I want to learn but never seem to get around to it." She shrugged. "Guess I'll put it on my bucket list." She pointed to Leighanne's near-empty can of paint. "Let me get you some more of that. Be right back."

Deborah traipsed to the collection of supplies across the room and returned with a can as Leighanne mused. Yes. Simple acceptance. She would miss that.

Her eyes strayed to the back of the room where Jamison stood with Arthur and Russell, two of the stage crew. Deep in conversation, his face was animated as he leaned toward the two men. His hands moved through the air as if conducting an orchestra. Arthur said something, and the trio broke into wild laughter.

Jamison clapped Russell on the back and turned in her

direction. His eyes met hers, and her breath caught. She suddenly understood the phrase "frozen like a deer in headlights." He grinned and touched his forehead in a playful salute then broke eye contact as one of the stage crew called his name.

She pressed her brush against the fake tree then realized she hadn't loaded the brush with more paint. With a sheepish laugh to herself, she squatted and dipped it into the can, glad for a distraction from her skittering pulse. She was supposed to be mad at him.

Deborah's voice broke in, "Have you known him long?"

"Who?"

"Jamison."

Leighanne daubed color onto the wood and spread it until her brush was dry. She was stalling, and she knew it. She didn't want to discuss her relationship, but Deborah looked at her in such expectation she replied, "Most of my life. His parents and mine were friends. How about you?"

"About three years. I met him at a soup kitchen where we were both serving. I was in a rough patch in my life, and he told me how God could make a difference. He invited me to his church. I was skeptical, but the sermon made me see how right he was. I accepted Jesus that day. It's not been a bed of roses, but I have a peace I never had before that." She blinked rapidly then flushed.

"I'm sorry. You probably didn't want to know my life story." She ducked her head and painted a few strokes on the prop.

"Don't be embarrassed. I appreciate hearing your testimony. I'm also a Christian."

Deborah beamed. "You are? That's wonderful! I never thought a successful actress like you could be a Christian."

Leighanne returned her smile, and they worked in silence for several minutes before Deborah began to hum *It is Well with My Soul* taking Leighanne back to her days at High Street Church. When was the last time she darkened the doorway of a sanctuary? She shuffled through her memories.

Too busy to go when she first arrived in New York, she attended the Christmas show at Radio City Music Hall the following year. The pageantry and glitter mesmerized her but not enough to send her searching for somewhere to worship. Then the play she was in added Sunday matinees, and the opportunity to look for a church disappeared like fog on a sunny day. It hadn't seemed as important as launching her career.

Did she have a career anymore? She was in England slapping paint on a plywood tree for an amateur production of *Robin Hood*. How far she had fallen!

Her eyes swept the room. Where was Jamison? The men he had been talking to were in the back of the room with the sound guy, a lanky twenty-something year old with wiry red hair and matching beard. Ears straining, she listened for Jamison's voice then wondered at her disappointment when she couldn't hear him.

Get a grip, Leighanne. You're here to help Kelli then get back to New York and try to resurrect your career. Your life with Jamison is over. He made that clear five years ago. Just because he's being nice doesn't mean he's in love with you again.

Finished with the tree, she stretched the stiffness from her back. The rest of the "forest" had stage crew working on them. Nothing remained for her to do at the moment. She looked at her paint-spattered fingers and arms and shook her head. Not the usual manicured look she wore.

"Nice working with you, Deborah. I'm going to wash up."

"You, too. Thanks again for helping us out."

"Sure thing."

Leighanne tossed the brush in the can, picked it up and padded off stage. She wandered down the hallway past several closed doors.

"I'm doing the best I can."

Leighanne stopped. Jamison. Where was he? She crept forward. The last door in the corridor was partially open, and she hesitated outside of it.

Jamison's voice came from within the room. "I'm well aware

the stakes in this. You don't have to remind me. She's here now...working on props...stage crew. We tried to run lines, but she nearly fainted. You...might happen..."

Silence.

Leighanne held her breath. He was talking about her. But to whom? What kind of stakes?

"I said I'd do it, and I will. Leave my sister out of this...I'll be in touch."

She heard him walk toward the door, and she gulped. It would not do to be caught. On soundless feet, she raced back the way she had come.

Chapter Seven

Jamison hung back from the group and shifted the heavy camera bag onto his shoulder. He always brought too many lenses when hiking, but the photographs he could capture with them made the discomfort worthwhile. However, the fifteen-minute walk from the car park seemed twice as long, thanks to the weight of the equipment.

One of the cast members arranged a field trip to Sherwood Forest to visit the Major Oak. He hadn't been back to see it since Leighanne left. Their favorite spot to picnic, it was too painful to visit without her. Now, staring at the majestic tree, the years faded away.

Leaning on the wooden rail fence, he searched through the foliage to find the scaffolding that supported the branches of the venerable tree. With a girth of over thirty-five feet, it reached more than fifty feet into the air, and its canopy stretched almost one hundred feet. He believed it when experts claimed it was nearly one thousand years old. An aura of age and wisdom surrounded the tree. Sure, there were other large oaks scattered through the forest, but this one was the granddaddy of them all.

He listened with half an ear as one of the women in the crowd gave a running monologue to her friend about the forest. She must be an American from somewhere in the southern part of their country – perhaps Georgia. Over the years of being docent at the castle, he made a game of learning to recognize the different accents from across the pond.

She spoke in hushed tones as if in a library. "They say Robin Hood and his men slept here. Can you imagine? About ten years ago, it was designated one of fifty Great British Trees. I can see why. It's magnificent, isn't it?"

Her companion gave a response he couldn't hear then she continued. "They had to erect the fence because the ground around the tree got so compressed from visitors' feet that it couldn't absorb water and nutrients."

The two moved away, and her voice faded. He set his satchel on the ground then rotated his neck to ease the kinks from his back. Bending, he unbuckled the straps that attached the tripod to the bag and unzipped it to retrieve his Nikon. He dug into the case to find a long-range lens and seated it on the camera. Fiddling with the knobs, he sent a surreptitious glance toward Leighanne.

Her body taut, she shielded her eyes with one hand. The sun

bounced off the blue-black tangle of her hair. She must also be caught in memories. From the look on her face, she was not too happy about it. Would she ever get over their breakup? His hands froze on the equipment. Maybe she still cared for him, and that's why she was angry. Doubtful, but a man could hope. Help me, Lord. I was a fool to let her go.

Shaking his head, he attached the camera to the tripod and backed away from the tree.

Forty minutes later, Jamison finished shooting pictures. The fading afternoon light had been perfect. He managed to push Leighanne out of his thoughts – well, mostly. He couldn't wait to get home to load the SD card on his computer and review the photos. Making quick work of stashing his equipment, he prayed, "Thank you for the beauty of this forest, Lord. I always feel so much closer to you among your creations. I love the bustle of town but enjoy the peaceful feeling I get outside."

He swung the satchel onto his shoulder and hummed *He Touched Me.* The cast members were scattered around the tree chatting. He wandered toward the fence encircling the tree and glanced at his watch. Not as late as he thought. Content to remain by himself, he set the bag on the ground and propped himself against the rails crossing his arms.

Several yards away, Leighanne stood with Kelli and one of the stage crew. From his peripheral vision he saw Leighanne look his way. The slight breeze carried bits and pieces of the women's conversation to him.

"...don't know....he meant that."

"you...talk...him."

"...can't be trusted..."

"Ask him."

The wind shifted, and Leighanne's next words came through loud and clear. "He said something about knowing what the stakes are. What could that mean?"

Jamison froze. She had been the one outside the room! Did she hear the entire conversation? What had he gotten himself into?

His lips moved as he softly prayed, "Lord, forgive me. I compromised my integrity when I agreed to Mr. Tillinghast's demands. I should have remembered you would take care of Lily and me, provide the finances we need for her medical care. Now I've hurt Leighanne in the process. She thinks...well...actually I don't know what she thinks. Help me, Lord."

He turned toward the mammoth tree and fell silent. Peace settled over him like gossamer. Smiling, he nodded. "Forgiven again. Thank you, Jesus."

Jamison wasn't sure how the situation would play out, but God was with him, and that's all that mattered. He scrubbed at his face then lifted his gaze to the branches dancing in the breeze. Yes, God was with him. He always had been. It was so easy to get caught up in the daily struggle and forget.

One day at a time, my son.

"I know, Lord. Thanks for the reminder." Jamison retrieved his gear from the ground and slung it over his shoulder. He shrugged to shift it to a more comfortable position then took a deep breath and approached the trio of women. "Stay as long as you want. There are still a couple of hours before we need to be back for rehearsal, but I'm done taking pictures and heading to the van."

He studiously avoided Leighanne's eyes, instead focusing on her sister. He couldn't read her expression either, but she seemed the safer choice.

"All right, Jamison. We won't be much longer." Kelli's voice held no emotion.

He gave her a brief nod and walked down the path toward the car park. As soon as he was out of earshot, he dug his cell phone from his pocket and dialed his boss. It rang several times before the man finally picked up.

"Hello?"

"Mr. Tillinghast? It's Jamison Blake. I'm calling to submit my resignation from the castle and the play. I can work until you find a replacement."

"Resignation? What? What's happened? Have you lost your mind? You gave me your word you would get that Webster woman on board so we could use the publicity to solicit more donors. You said you were a Christian. Do Christians go back on their word, Blake?"

"That's just it, sir. I can't compromise my beliefs to strong arm Leighanne into taking the lead. I never should have promised you I would. I'll have to figure out another way to pay for my sister's medical bills, but I can't do what you've asked of me, sir. You'll need to find someone else..."

"I will find someone else—someone who is willing to play by my terms. I should have known you couldn't be trusted. I'll inform the board of directors about your actions, and you'll find it tough to secure another job in this town." The phone clicked, and the man was gone.

Jamison arrived at the van and unlocked the back. Swinging open both doors, he stowed his things then seated himself on the floor, legs dangling over the bumper. He stared off into the distance. "What have I done?"

Chapter Eight

A knock thudded on the door to Kelli's flat. Sitting on the couch, Leighanne stuffed a bookmark into the travel guide she was reading and looked at her watch. Who could be here at 8:30 in the morning?

The rapping repeated, and she inventoried her appearance. Not exactly appropriate to entertain a guest - torn SUNY sweatshirt, faded jeans, and fuzzy red slippers. She could only imagine what her hair looked like, but at least she had brushed her teeth.

She set the book on the table at her elbow and swung her feet over the edge of the sofa. "Just a minute!" Avoiding the mirror on the way to the door, she tugged her sweatshirt down over her hips before closing one eye to peek through the peephole. She reared back and clapped a hand over her mouth to squelch the gasp that erupted.

Jamison!

What did he want? Her mind raced. He couldn't see her like

this. What would he think? Wait a minute. Did it matter what he thought? He was up to no good, and it involved her in some way.

She stiffened then yanked open the door. "Hello, Jamison. What can I do for you?"

"Uh, may I come in? We need to talk."

He was pale, and lines marred his face. Dark smudges rimmed his bloodshot eyes. He still wore yesterday's outfit. Was he hung over? She stared at him, her mouth agape.

"Leighanne? Are you going to let me in?"

Footsteps sounded behind her, and she looked over her shoulder to see her sister enter the living room. In tan slacks and a mint green blouse, Kelli had swept the sides of her hair into mother-of-pearl combs and left the back hanging free. Leighanne sagged against the door. She was the ugly duckling in comparison.

Kelli said, "Who is it?"

Leighanne swung the door wider. "It's Jamison." She mouthed to her sister, "I think he's been drinking."

Kelli rushed forward, anxiety evident on her face. "Come in, Jamison. Are you okay? Can I get you some tea? The kettle should only take a few moments to heat up."

Jamison walked past, and Leighanne sniffed the air. No tangy scent of alcohol. Why did he look so awful? Was he ill?

She closed the door and followed him to her recently vacated couch. The electric kettle gurgled from the kitchen. Cabinets and drawers banged as Kelli retrieved a mug and associated tea-making supplies. Leighanne shifted from one foot to the other. Should she excuse herself to change her clothes? No. Then he would think she was trying to impress him. She dropped onto the far end of the sofa and waited for him to speak. Despite his ragged appearance, he seemed content to sit in silence.

She leaned back and crossed her arms. Fine. She'd wait him out.

Kelli's heels clicked on the hardwood floor as she entered the room carrying a steaming cup of tea. She handed it to Jamison with a caution, "Careful, it's hot."

Lowering herself into a nearby chair, she looked at Leighanne who shrugged. Jamison blew on the aromatic liquid then sipped quietly, his Adam's apple bobbing as he swallowed. He closed his eyes for a brief moment and moaned, "Delicious." He smiled at Kelli. "Exactly what I needed. Thanks for seeing me."

Kelli leaned forward and patted his knee. "Of course. Is everything all right? Are you sick?"

He shook his head and gave a mirthless laugh. "I look a fright, I know. It's been a long night. I believe I know how Joseph felt when he wrestled with the angel of God."

"And you came to tell us about it?"

"Yes. And I couldn't wait another minute." He rubbed his unshaven jaw and gestured to his clothes. "Maybe I should have cleaned up a bit first."

Kelli shook her head. "Friends don't stand on ceremony. Isn't that right, Leighanne?"

Unsure what to make of Jamison, Leighanne nodded. He seemed different than yesterday, but she couldn't put her finger on what it was. "Uh, sure. You don't look much worse than I do."

His face softened as he met her eyes. "I don't know what you mean. You look lovely. You always do."

Her face flushed, and she wiped her moist palms on her pants as she dropped her eyes. What was she doing getting all doe-eyed at him? He was playing her. She had heard him on the phone. He was definitely up to something. She tried to get Kelli's attention, but her sister was focused on Jamison.

Leighanne picked up her mug, the tea having lost its warmth long ago. She rubbed her thumb along the rim and stared at the amber liquid. Jamison set his drink down with a thunk and sat back with a deep sigh. "Thanks, Kelli. That was spot on."

He leaned forward, his forearms resting on his thighs. Color had returned to his face, and the dark circles under his eyes had faded. "Thank you for seeing me. I owe you both an apology and an explanation." He stared intently at Leighanne. "I know you heard my telephone conversation, and you're upset. You have every right to be."

Embarrassment at being caught eavesdropping and anger at being the target of the conversation warred within her. Then his earnest expression touched her, and she gave him an imperceptible nod. "I'm listening."

Relief swept across his face. "Thank you." He cleared his throat and closed his eyes for a brief moment. "When my parents were killed in the car accident three years ago, I discovered Dad's printing business was failing and had been for several years. He and Mum had taken a second mortgage out on the house, but were having trouble making the payment. They also owed money to nearly everyone with whom they did business."

He paused to take a sip from his mug. "We lost the house. Lily and I couldn't come up with the past due amount. We could have walked away from the other debt but didn't feel right about that, so we arranged to make monthly payments to the creditors. It's been tight, but we've managed.

"Then six months ago, we discovered that Lily has a heart defect that must be repaired. Apparently, it's always been there. We're not sure why the doctors never detected it. She's on the list for surgery, but it could take more than a year for her to reach the front of the line. We've found a doctor in America who will do the surgery, but we have to make a down payment. Meanwhile we continue to accrue more debt because of doctors' appointments and tests."

He blew out his breath, and his eyes glistened with unshed tears. "Paying off the debt is taking every extra pence we make. We haven't been able to save anything toward the operation. We prayed for God to provide the funds, and I thought he had when my boss came to me with a deal."

Pain marred his visage. "But now I see I was wrong to agree to what Mr. Tillinghast wanted. And I'm sorry to have dragged you into my problems."

Confusion filled Leighanne. "I don't understand how my being here is a solution to your financial situation."

Mr. Tillinghast wants to leverage your name to solicit donations for his foundation, and that would be easier to do if you were in the play, rather than just co-producing with Kelli. He wants you to play Maid Marian."

Leighanne shuddered. "You don't think he caused Louise's accident, do you? To take her out of the part?"

Kelli bolted upright. "Leighanne, that's quite an accusation. Mr. Tillinghast is a leading business man in our community."

"I'm just saying..."

Jamison held up his hands. "That sort of thing may happen in

New York, but not here in Nottingham. I don't think he had anything to do with her accident, but he is savvy enough to take advantage of the situation. He had already planned to use your name when you were producing."

"Do you really think my association with this will translate into a significant amount of money?"

He shrugged. "Mr. Tillinghast apparently does. He is willing to pay the entire amount of Lily's operation if I can get you to do it. I told him I'd use our past...uh...relationship to make it happen. But I've realized that's wrong. And I've been running ahead of the Lord. I know he's going to provide for Lily and me, and I won't have to use subterfuge for it to happen."

He rubbed at the stubble on his face then ran his fingers through his hair. "Can you forgive me?"

Lily's face came to Leighanne's mind. Sweet, gentle Lily who saw the good in everyone, who had ensured every new kid at school was welcomed with open arms, who had more than once put another person's needs ahead of her own.

Leighanne smiled as she remembered the time Kelly and Lily had joined her on the London Eye. Leighanne had accepted the dare from Fran what's-her-name, the school bully, but was too proud to admit her fear of heights and back down. The girls had tagged along and kept her spirits up during the tortuous thirty minute ride. They had giggled and talked the whole time to keep her from focusing on the distance to the ground, especially when they reached the top. Afterwards they had joined elbows with her as she wobbled off on rubbery legs, waving at Fran as if it had been no big deal.

Tears threatened as the memory faded. "I'll do it."

"What?" Kelli and Jamison spoke at the same time.

"I'll play the part of Maid Marian. Lily has always been there for me, even after you and I...well, you know. If that's all I have to do to get your Mr. Tillinghast to cough up the money for Lily's surgery, then I'll do it. Besides, you still haven't found anyone else to do it."

Jamison shook his head. "I can't ask you to do that. God will provide without us bowing to Tillinghast's demands."

"Maybe this is how God is providing, Jamison."

Kelli rubbed Leighanne's knee. "Are you sure?"

Sweat sprang out on her upper lip, but Leighanne she set her jaw. "I've never been more certain of anything in my life."

Jamison moved from the chair to kneel in front of her. He grasped her cold, clammy hands in his warm ones. "God loves you, Leighanne, and he's going to get you through this. It will be as if you never had panic attacks. I know it." He glanced at Kelli then back at her. "We'll pray you through every moment."

His cell phone rang, and Leighanne extricated her hands. He fumbled for the phone in his pocket and looked at the display. "It's the hospital."

Chapter Nine

Jamison barged through the front door of the hospital and rushed into the lobby. He wrinkled his nose then coughed at the cloying antiseptic aroma inside the facility. His soles slapped against the tile floor as he turned into the nearest hallway and race-walked toward his sister's room. No need to waste time getting yelled at by the nursing staff for running.

His breath was ragged in his ears when he stopped in the doorway to Lily's room. He bent, hands on his knees, and inhaled deeply before letting out his breath. In. Out. In. Out. He righted himself and peeked inside.

Sleeping Beauty. Her eyes were closed, her lashes dark against her porcelain complexion that was nearly translucent. Someone had wrapped her waist length blonde hair into two braids, and her hands lay clasped on top of the white blanket. Her right index finger was encased in a plastic monitor whose cord snaked across her shoulder to the machine behind her head. Its muted beeps were the only sound in the room.

He tiptoed forward and lowered himself into the molded plastic chair next to the bed. The seat creaked, and he froze. When she didn't awaken, he bowed his head. He had talked to God all the way from Kelli's flat to the hospital, but it had been the ravings of a desperate man. Now that he could see Lily resting comfortably, he needed to thank his heavenly Father and apologize for his lack of faith...again.

Bowing his head, he prayed through stiff lips, "Thank you, Father. You have taken care of Lily again. And me. I'm sorry for my disbelief. You shower us with blessings day after day, and yet when there is one bump in the road, I fail to trust you. Forgive me, Father. I have failed to believe in your sovereignty again. You must be so tired of me. I know I am. Take care of Lily, Lord. Only you can heal her – whether through a miracle or through the wonders of science. I don't want to lose her. She's the only family I have left."

Leighanne's face flashed into his mind. "Thank you for Leighanne's willingness to play Maid Marian. Take away her fear. Heal her panic attacks. Help her depend on you, and bless her for her selfless gift to Lily so Mr. Tillinghast will pay for the surgery."

Jamison fell quiet and let the peace of God wash over him. His shoulders relaxed, and his hands unclenched in his lap. Light filled his soul, and hope bloomed within his chest. Why did he always let himself get tied into knots?

A feathery touch tickled his arm. He opened his eyes to find Lily watching him, her emerald green eyes bright, and a smile on her face. She licked her lips, and he jumped up to pour water from the bedside pitcher into one of the cups next to it. He braced her against his shoulder and held the drink to her lips. She took several sips before pushing his hand away.

He lowered her back against the pillow then set the cup on the table before searching her face. "Is there anything else I can get you? Do you need the nurse? Are you in pain?"

"Sit down. I'm fine." She gave him a crooked grin. "Well, as fine as I can be without being allowed out of here."

"You gave us quite a scare."

Still grinning, she said, "I gave me quite a scare."

"It's nothing to laugh about. I'm grateful it was angina and not a heart attack. We could have lost you."

"And I would have been in a better place."

"Yes. But I would have missed you desperately. You're too young to die."

"God does not guarantee us a long life, Jamison. You know that. My death may be for a greater good."

Fear gripped him. "That's where your faith is stronger than mine, little sister. But enough talk of death because I have excellent news."

He sat back and crossed his arms.

Lily giggled, "You're going to make me guess, aren't you?"

He nodded.

"It's not going to be hard. I heard you praying. Leighanne is going to act in the play which means Mr. Tillinghast will hold up his end of the bargain and pay for my surgery."

Jamison reached over and held her hand. "Isn't that wonderful?"

She gave him a hard stare. "Only if it isn't harmful to Leighanne."

"What do you mean?"

"Her panic attacks. Maybe she's not ready to be back on stage, even for our little production. It is not fair to ask her to do this just so I can have surgery. God is going to provide." "She told me she is God's provision."

Lily rolled onto her side to face him and tucked her left arm under her cheek. "She said that?"

"Yes. I can tell she's afraid, but she wants to do this for you. She said she was never more certain of anything in her life. And I've decided to rescind my resignation if Mr. Tillinghast will accept it. Leighanne loves you, Lily, and she's willing to risk everything for you. "

"Maybe, but I think she's doing it because she still loves you, Jamison."

Jamison shook his head. "How can you say that? She was going to drop out and return to America when she found out I was the director."

Lily looked resolute. "That was fear. I'm sure of it."

"Fear of what? She didn't know she was going to be in the limelight."

"Her feelings for you. Remember, you're the one who broke off the relationship. She's never dated anyone since she left. I think it's because she's never gotten over you."

"I don't..."

Lily lifted her head. "And you're still in love with her. Are you going to let her go back to America without telling her? Do you love her enough to give her up?"

Jamison rubbed his eyes with the heels of his hands then slumped in the chair. "I have to."

"Why?"

"I..."

"Why can't you join her in New York? You could get a job in one of their museums. Sure, you'd have to get a visa and all that, but it would be worth it. Don't you think?"

"You're certainly full of plans and ideas, aren't you, little sister."

Lily rolled onto her back with a huff. "That's all I can do, stuck in this bed all day and night. Think and pray. Pray and think. Not that I mind the praying so much, but I do feel a bit useless. A burden, really."

Jamison jumped up and hugged his sister then released her and stared into her eyes. "Don't ever say that again. Do you hear me? I don't know what I'd do without you. You are not a burden and never will be. Your love, your support, your encouragement...they mean the world to me. And we're going to get you out of here. Once you have the surgery, you'll be as good as new."

She closed her eyes, and a tear slid down her right cheek as she whispered, "I hope so. I don't know how much longer I can wait. I feel as if God has forgotten me, Jamison."

He embraced her again as she sobbed, wetting the front of his shirt with her sorrow. Stroking her hair, he murmured soothing words in her ear. What could he do? How could he bring light to her? Help me, Lord...no...help Lily. Touch her. Let her feel your presence. You heard her.

A knock sounded at the door, and the two drew apart. A nurse entered the room, her shoes squeaking on the tile floor. She moved to the far side of the bed and lifted Lily's arm to take her pulse.

Compassion filled her coffee-colored face. "Are you in pain, Miss Blake?"

Lily used the sheet to dab the wetness from her face. "No."

Jamison laced his fingers together. "It's been a long stay."

The nurse laid her hand on Lily's forehead. "A bit downhearted, are you? Perhaps I have some news that will perk you up." She tapped her clipboard. "These are orders from your doctor in America. He needs a couple of tests done since your angina attack. Depending on the results, your surgery may get pushed forward. Now, you rest. The orderlies will be in shortly to take you downstairs."

A tentative smile formed on Lily's lips, and Jamison clapped his hands. "That's a mixed blessing. Isn't it, Nurse?"

The nurse looked at the two of them. "Yes. It would mean there has been more damage to the heart."

Chapter Ten

The sun warmed her back as Leighanne stood with Kelli in front of Newstead Abbey. She peered at the stone building and listened to Kelli's monologue about its history.

"Can you believe this place is over eight hundred and fifty years old? It was a priory in the early days then Henry VIII gave it to Sir John Byron in 1540. Over two hundred and fifty years later, it passed to the poet Lord Byron. He lived here intermittently between 1808 and 1814, when he sold it. As you can imagine, it cost a fortune in upkeep."

"I had no idea it was so huge." Leighanne looked at her watch. "Will we have time to see the gardens, too?"

"We can do that first, if you'd like."

"I would. I'm not complaining, but there's been an awful lot of rain. It's nice to be outside for a change."

Kelly gave her a wry grin. "Sure, you're not complaining."

Leighanne nudged her shoulder. "Okay, maybe a tiny bit."

They wandered along the path around the abbey and arrived at the Garden Lake. Kelli read from the brochure, "The lake was created by Thomas Wildman in about 1820 and bordered by specimens of swamp cypress, Luscombe oak and willow. More recent plantings include a memorial swamp cypress planted in 1988 by the Mayor of Missolonghi, the Greek town where the poet Byron died in 1824."

Movement across the water caught Leighanne's attention, and she pointed to a grey heron flexing its wings. She lowered her voice. "Not too many of those in New York City. He's magnificent."

Kelli nodded, and the two watched him for several minutes before continuing along the path that paralleled the lake.

The women shared a laugh then ambled to the end of the lane where they turned toward the French Garden. Kelli cast an eye at the sky as she pointed to the sundial in the middle of the graveled walks. "Do you know how to read one of these things?"

Gesturing to the blade-like piece in the center of the dial, Leighanne said, "That's called a gnomon, and its edges are called styles. When the sun hits it, the shadow will tell you what time it is."

Kelli stared at her, and Leighanne laughed. "It's amazing what sort of flotsam you pick up over the years in the entertainment industry."

They stood for several minutes drinking in the beauty of the foliage. Kelli gave Leighanne a quick one-armed hug. "Thanks for what you're doing for Lily Blake. It means a lot."

Leighanne nodded without looking at her sister. "It's hard to say no to her."

"She would never want you to do something you weren't comfortable with."

"I know. I meant it's hard to say no to the idea of her needing help. If I had the money, I'd give it to her. I may be fairly well-known, but that doesn't translate into the kind of cash movie stars make. I make a good salary, but I haven't saved anywhere near the amount she needs."

"But Tillinghast has it."

"Yeah, but what he's doing feels a bit like blackmail, you know?"

The duo fell silent, and Leighanne walked to a granite bench a short distance away. Kelli followed her, and they seated themselves on the cold stone.

Leighanne spoke at a whisper, "He's so different now."

"Jamison?"

"He's always had a quiet strength, but it's deeper somehow. I don't know how to explain it."

"It's his faith. When their parents died, he spun out of control. Angry. Hateful. Drinking a lot. But Lily brought him back from the dark. She asked me to pray about it with her. So, we prayed. Every day. God finally broke through."

"What happened?"

Kelli shook her head. "It's his story to tell, and he will if you ask him. His faith is what you're seeing now."

"He's been a Christian as long as I can remember. What changed?"

"Like I said, he can tell you exactly what happened. He hit bottom, and God pulled him out of the mire. That changes a person. He'll be the first to say he's not perfect, but his dependence on God shapes everything he does."

Leighanne's brow wrinkled. "Then why did he get sucked in Tillinghast's offer."

"Desperation? Don't you remember how we were when Mom and Dad both got sick so close together? It was awful. We would have done anything to make them better."

"You're right. I still don't understand why God chose to take them both away from us, but I don't blame Him for it anymore. Although I must admit, I struggle with trusting Him sometimes."

"We all do."

"Not like me. Do you find yourself waiting for God to yank the rug out from under you? I do. Especially when things are going well. I start looking over my shoulder, wondering when the good times are going to fall apart. And I know that's not how God operates. He's not capricious like that, but I still feel that way nonetheless."

"Oh, Leighanne. I had no idea you had these kind of difficulties."

"How could you? I'm over three thousand miles away."

Kelly shrugged, "We're sisters. Shouldn't I have had some inkling? A sense that something was wrong?"

"Maybe you did. You invited me over, remember?"

Kelli's face brightened. "True enough. And we're together now."

"Thanks for listening and not judging me, Kell."

"Who am I to judge? I've argued and disobeyed God on more than one occasion." She laughed, "Not that I'm going to give you specifics, mind you."

Leighanne grinned. "Turnabout's fair play. I told you my issues."

"We don't have that kind of time, sis. Maybe..."

The strains of Beethoven's Ninth Symphony came from deep inside Kelli's purse. "Drat. I was hoping we could have the afternoon to ourselves. It has been wonderful to reconnect like this." She pulled her pocketbook off her shoulder, unzipped it and reached inside to rummage for her cell phone. "Remind me again why I carry so much stuff."

Leighanne pointed to the leather pouched strapped around her own waist. "You're asking me? A woman who uses a belly-bag just big enough for a phone, a tube of lipstick and a few bucks. I have no idea why you cart that suitcase around."

Kelli continued to root around in her satchel, and the music quit. "Oh, bother! Now I've missed the call. Aha! Here you are, you silly thing." With a look of triumph, she held up her phone then peered at the display. "Tom Haddonfield. Wonder what he needs."

"Call him back. It will only take a minute, and you'll feel better."

Kelli fiddled with the buttons, mumbling to herself. She looked at Leighanne with chagrin. "I'm a technological imbecile. I never remember how to dial the last call that came in."

Leighanne reached for the phone. "You have other gifts." She punched a couple of buttons and handed the device back to her sister. "It's ringing."

Holding the phone to her ear, Kelli said, "Thanks. You'd think...Hello, Tom...it's Kelli. Sorry I missed...what...the costumes? When? Okay. I'll be right there." She pressed a key on the phone and dropped it back into the recesses of her bag. "We've got to go. Tom went over to the rehearsal hall to finish up on the arrows and found that someone had left the window open in the prop room.

Thanks to last night's rainstorm, we've got a pile of drenched costumes. They could be ruined."

Chapter Eleven

Jamison sat cross-legged on the grass, his back propped against the boulder near the lake. He checked his watch then closed his eyes. He still had a couple of hours before visitation started at the hospital. The sun warmed him, and the breeze brushed his face. The scent of some flower hovered in the air.

A woman and two children dawdled at the edge of the water, tearing off bits of bread from a small loaf and tossing them into the water. The surface churned as fish fought to gobble up the food. Several hundred yards away, a gray-haired man sat in a canvas chair, a rod and reel in his hands. He periodically threw the line then cranked it back in. Didn't he realize his prey were being fed down here?

Footsteps sounded, and he looked up to see a pair of joggers in matching hunter-orange sweatsuits.

He should be home updating his resume and hunting the online job boards for his next position. Too bad he wasn't a high-powered executive. He would call a couple of search firms and have them do the work for him. Yeah, that was going to happen.

What did Leighanne do to find a new job? As far as he could tell, there were hundreds, if not thousands, of actors and actresses who all wanted to be in the next greatest film or television show or play. She had mentioned an agent. It must be his or her responsibility to find the opportunities.

He hadn't expected to work at the castle forever, but having to look for a new job every few months would be difficult. Every year or two if a long-running gig came along would be too often. What gave Leighanne her desire to be on stage? To have all those people staring at her.

The stone dug into his back, and moisture from the grass seeped through his pants. Shaking his head to clear the image of her face from his mind, he got to his feet and began to amble along the brick path that encircled the small body of water.

Jamison squinted against the dazzling sunlight and fumbled in his shirt pocket for his sunglasses. He slid them over his eyes then shoved his hands into the front pockets of his jeans. His sneakers were soundless except for the periodic pebble they kicked up along the way.

He passed a jungle-gym crawling with young children while a crowd of adults clustered nearby. He stopped to watch the kids, smiling at their dare-devil antics. His watch pinged, and he pressed the button on the side to shut off the alarm. Break time was over. His next job would not find itself.

Crossing the grassy knoll, he made his way to the car. He unlocked it and dropped into the front seat. He glanced over at his cell phone he had left in the vehicle. Seeing the missed call indicator, he broke out into a sweat. He swiped his finger over the display and breathed a sigh of relief when the phone list showed the call had not come from the hospital, but from Tillinghast.

What did he want?

Jamison poked at the screen to bring up his voicemail, but the box was empty. Should he call him back? And ruin a peaceful afternoon? No. The man could call back.

As if conjured up, Tillinghast's number appeared on the screen. Jamison held the vibrating device in his hand, torn about what to do. Did he want to hash out whatever the man had to say? On the fourth ring, Jamison swiped at the "answer" icon and lifted the phone to his ear.

"Hello, this is Jamison."

"Blake, Charles Tillinghast here. Have I caught you at a bad time?"

"No, sir. What can I do for you?"

Jamison moved the phone away from his head, and the man's bombastic voice filled the car. "It's what I can do for you."

"And what is that, sir?"

"Take the pressure off you about Miss Webster. I may have been out of line in asking you to persuade her to take the role of Maid Marian."

Jamison sat up and stared at the phone, mouth working as he tried to come up with a response.

"Are you there, son?"

"Ah, yessir, I'm here."

"Good. I was talking with my wife. You remember my wife, Penelope, don't you? Anyway, we were talking about the festival and the play and all that, and she said that Miss Webster had probably come to England for a break, and here we were asking her to take on a role within the production itself. And that's not good form, is it?"

"Ah, no sir."

"Glad to hear we're on the same page. So, you can just forget our little conversation about convincing her join the cast."

Jamison cleared his throat. "There's only one problem, Mr. Tillinghast. Leighanne...I mean Miss Webster has already agreed to play Maid Marian."

Silence filled the car, and it was Jamison's turn to say, "Are you still there?"

"That's a problem."

"I beg your pardon, sir?"

"You need to figure out how to get her to un-agree."

Jamison wiped a hand over his face. "But I thought you wanted her name in lights, as it were. So, that we might get a bigger audience and more donations. Don't you remember? I'm no longer part of the production."

"You said you'd help until I found a replacement. Now you don't need to quit after all. You didn't think she'd want to be on stage. Now, she doesn't have to. Tell her we've found someone to be Maid Marian."

"And who would that be?"

"I don't know. That's your job."

"Why the sudden change of heart, sir? What aren't you telling me?"

Tillinghast's voice rose an octave. "I'm sure I don't know what you mean."

Realization dawned on Jamison, and he spoke with fervor. "You heard about Leighanne's panic attacks. You think she won't be able to handle being on stage, and that could ruin your big plans. That's it, isn't it?"

A heavy sigh came through the phone. "Surely, you understand my position, Mr. Blake. I've been tasked to look out for the good of the castle. The embarrassment of a washed up actress having a panic attack on stage isn't the kind of press we need right now."

Jamison spoke through clenched teeth. "Leighanne is not washed up. She agreed to take the part, and I believe she can do it."

"I don't understand you, Blake. You're getting what you wanted, and now you're telling me it's not what you want. I'm giving you your job back, and you don't have to force Miss Webster into playing a role she is not fit for."

"But she is fit for it. That's what I'm saying. Yes, Leighanne had some issues in New York, but she's over them."

"I'm not convinced. She hasn't been here long enough to be 'over them' as you say. So, here's the deal – you keep your job, you notify Miss Webster her services are not needed, and your sister gets her financing."

Jamison took a deep breath then said in a rush, "No thank you, Mr. Tillinghast. Lily and I will find another way to get the funding for her surgery. I can't, in good conscience, tell Leighanne we don't need her in order to keep my job. God will provide. I just need to trust Him on that."

"I hope that works out for you, Blake." Sarcasm dripped from the man's voice. "Meanwhile, I'll have the personal things from your office couriered to you."

"That's very generous, Mr. Tillinghast, but it's no trouble to go pick them up."

"You're not understanding me, Blake. You can continue to direct the play, but your employment is terminated. As of this moment, you're not allowed back in the castle."

Chapter Twelve

Leighanne raked her fingers through her hair then threw the script onto the coffee table. She dropped onto the couch in Kelli's flat and leaned back to stare at the ceiling. How was she ever going to memorize these lines?

Was exhaustion the problem? She and Kelli had worked well into the evening with Tom to clean up the mess in the prop room and to assess the damage to the costumes. She had wrung water out of clothes until her arms ached and her fingers were prunes. Despite several doses of lotion, they were still wrinkled and dry.

Was fear creating her inability to learn the words? She paused, waiting for the familiar grip of her palpating heart and sweaty palms to overtake her. When these constant companions did not arrive at the thought of stepping out on stage, she grinned then bit her lip. No need to get cocky. Just because she wasn't having a panic attack now didn't mean they were gone for good.

Was it Jamison? Jamison. Warmth filled her. What was up with that?

She closed her eyes and prayed, "Lord, I could use some help here. I don't know what to do about him. You know how important my career is to me. His life is here, and mine is in New York. Besides, he's the one who dumped me. Why would he follow me across the pond? He seems to care for me at some level, but is it love, or is he just being nice to an old friend?"

Leighanne opened her eyes and leaned forward, lacing her fingers together. The heady fragrance from the roses on the coffee table filled the room. The vase had been on the front porch when they arrived home. They had come without a card. Next to the flowers lay the script. She sighed. Back to square one. Why couldn't she get these lines into her head?

The shower in Kelli's bathroom ceased, and Leighanne could hear her sister bumping around behind the closed door. The hair dryer roared for several moments then the door opened, and her sister emerged in a cloud of steam. Her baby blue flannel pajama pants peeked out from under her white fleece robe. Fuzzy blue slippers completed her outfit.

Kelli shuffled across the room and flounced into the upholstered chair that was catty-corner from the couch. She propped her feet on the coffee table and jerked her head toward the script. "How's it going?"

Leighanne frowned. "Not so good. I'm beginning to regret my

agreement. I can't retain the words."

Kelli gave her an encouraging smile. "It will come. You've got a lot on your mind, and you must be worn out. What possessed you to try to run lines tonight anyway?" She glanced at the small clock on the mantle. "It's nearly ten o'clock. No one can remember anything at ten o'clock at night."

"You forget this is normally the middle of my day. When I'm in a production, we're still on stage at this hour. I don't usually get to bed until two or three o'clock."

Kelli yawned broadly. "This is way past my bed time. I almost fell asleep in the shower."

Leighanne patted Kelli's knee. "That's because you're up before the birds. It all works out. You should turn in. Get some rest. We've got another long day tomorrow."

As she rose, Kelli pointed to the roses. "I guess you're used to getting anonymous flowers. I think it's kind of creepy."

Leighanne shrugged. "The cast members have been friendly. Maybe they went in on it together."

Kelli shook her head. "They would have signed the card. This definitely has all the makings of a secret admirer." She snapped her fingers and said, "Maybe they're from Jamison. He still loves you, you know."

"I don't think so."

"You don't think they're from Jamison, or you don't think he's still in love with you?"

Leighanne grimaced. "Both."

"Then I guess we've got a mystery on our hands."

Chapter Thirteen

Jamison's sneakers crunched on the packed ground as he jogged along the tree lined path. It was a great day for a jog, and he was in the zone. Non-runners didn't understand. The pure joy of a good run—the feel of the ground beneath his feet, the air coming into his lungs and expelling in rhythmic perfection, the tension in his muscles.

He nodded to the guy coming toward him. Dressed in cotton shorts and a faded T-shirt with expensive running shoes and a wire that snaked from the buds in his ears to the music player strapped to his upper arm, the man nodded in return. No need to speak.

Jamison preferred to listen to God's creation as he ran – the chirps and birdsong filled the branches above his head, the chipmunks and squirrels skittered among the foliage on the ground. His problems didn't seem as overwhelming when he was on the trail. He understood why Jesus separated himself from the disciples periodically. Not that he could compare himself to his Lord.

As much as he loved working at the castle, the politics of trying to please everyone chipped away at his peace. Maybe being fired was the right answer.

His cell phone rang, and he yanked it from his pocket. Normally he didn't answer while running, but it could be the hospital. He glanced at the display. Kelli Webster. This could be interesting. He swiped at the screen to answer the call.

"Hey, Kelli. What's up?"

"Did you send flowers to Leighanne?"

"What?"

"You heard me." Her voice was strident. "Leighanne got a bouquet of flowers, but there was no card. Are they from you?"

"Why are you angry with me?"

"You didn't answer the question, Jamison."

He stopped on the trail. So much for peace. "No, I didn't send the flowers. Why would I do that?"

"Don't lie to me, Jamison."

"I'm not lying!"

"What kind of game are you playing?"

Jamison looked at the phone in his hand for a moment then replied, "What are you talking about? I'm not playing any games."

Nothing.

"Kelli? Are you there?"

The line was dead. She had hung up.

Chapter Fourteen

Moisture slicked Leighanne's palms as she gripped the script. Jamison lay on the stage, his eyes rolled back in his head. He was demonstrating what he wanted in the last scene where Robin Hood dies as the result of an ambush. Silence filled the air. It was her turn to speak, and she couldn't find her place on the page.

Her eyes bounced over the blurry words in front of her. Lord, I could use some help here. I can't have another panic attack. I'm no good to these people or to Lily if I can't do this. Are you there, Lord?

She closed her eyes for a moment and counted to ten. When she opened her eyes, she found Jamison looking at her with apprehension. She gave him a faltering smile, and he screwed up his face and clutched his abdomen as if in great pain then winked before heaving a huge sigh as his head lolled to one side.

Her smile widened, and the tension drained from her shoulders. She looked down at the script and found her place.

Thank you, Lord.

She fell to her knees next to Jamison. "Robin! Robin! You can't leave me. What will I ever do without you?" She dropped her head onto his chest, and his hand came up and stroked her hair. She shivered at the touch. Focus, Leighanne. It doesn't mean anything.

With a raspy voice, Jamison/Robin said, "Always remember, Marian. I love you..."

Leighanne/Marian lifted her head, and tears streamed down her face. "Sleep well, my sweet Robin Hood. You will be avenged."

The two held their pose for a moment, and the cast applauded wildly as they whistled and cheered. Leighanne's face warmed, and she wiped the wetness from her cheeks. Jamison gave her a long look before he jumped up and took an exaggerated bow. He bent to grasp her hand and gently pulled her to her feet. The troupe continued to clap, and he drew her close in a quick hug as he whispered in her ear. "See, I knew you could do it. You were wonderful."

He released her and made a sweeping motion with his arm indicating she should bow. She dropped a brief curtsy and grinned at him. Rehearsals never felt like this in New York.

Jamison raised his voice. "All right, people. I think that's enough for tonight. There's a school group coming through tomorrow, so we need to put everything away."

The babble of voices was broken by the clatter and clunks of props being moved. Kelli trotted up the stairs from the pit and made a beeline for Jamison and Leighanne. Her face glowed. "You two were amazing. Like you were actually Robin and Marian."

Jamison chuckled, "Don't sound so surprised, Kelli. After all, your sister is a professional."

Kelli pinked, and Jamison nudged her with his shoulder. "Kidding. I'm kidding you."

Leighanne tucked her script under her left arm. "Ignore him, Kell. He's been angling for a fight all night."

Kelli said, "He's going to get one if he's not careful."

Jamison's face was the picture of innocence. "What's that supposed to mean?"

"Excuse us, coming through."

The trio jumped out of the way as several of the crew marched through with trees from the wooden forest. Kelli pointed to the seating. "Maybe we'd be safer over there."

Leighanne and Jamison followed her down the stairs, and she led them to a secluded corner of the auditorium. Jamison crossed his arms and narrowed his eyes. "Okay, Kelli, what gives?"

"I want to have this out once and for all. Did you send flowers to Leighanne?"

"Kelli!" Leighanne gaped at her sister.

"What? I don't want him to hurt you again."

Jamison blew out his breath. "There wasn't a card?"

"No."

"I promise you, I didn't send any flowers. If I had, they would have been black-eyed Susans – your favorite."

Leighanne smiled and dropped her eyes. He remembered.

Kelli frowned. "Then who sent them? If it was someone we know, there would have been a card. It's creepy."

Jamison exchanged a look with Leighanne. His eyes clouded. "Does this happen often?"

She shrugged, "More than the security guards would like. To be honest, it's such mayhem back stage, the cards can easily fall off. Of course, that's not the case here. I think Kelli's making more of it than necessary. It's probably one of the cast members who's shy."

He crossed his arms and looked mulish. "I might believe that if it had only been one bouquet. But a second one? We should call the police."

Leighanne shook her head. "Absolutely not. We have no way of knowing which florist they're from. Even if we did, I'll bet they were paid for in cash. I haven't been harmed. Let's drop it."

Kelli snorted, "See what I'm up against?"

"She's got a point about having nothing for the police to go on.

How about if we make her promise never to be alone?"

Leighanne waved her hands in the air. "Hello! I can hear you. Could you not talk about me like I'm not here?"

Jamison's face flushed, "Sorry. But are you willing to have someone with you at all times? Are you okay with that?"

"Yes, but only because I know neither of you are going to let this rest if I don't agree."

Kelli hugged her. "Thanks, sis. I know you think we're overreacting, but we're not used to this sort of thing. And I don't know what I'd do if something happened to you."

Leighanne hung her head. "I guess I've been on my own too long."

"Leighanne?"

The trio looked up to see one of the cast members coming toward them. In his arms, he held a massive bouquet of flowers.

Chapter Fifteen

Two days later, Jamison herded a tour group to the front of Nottingham Contemporary, their footsteps echoing against the sidewalk. Some of the cast members had joined them, Leighanne included. He tried not to stare, but found his eyes straying toward her more often than not. Fortunately, she seemed oblivious, or maybe she was acting. He hadn't told the girls about being fired, but Kelli would find out at work soon enough.

He gestured toward the scalloped building, "Before we go inside, be sure to look closely at the lace pattern on the panels. It is a traditional panel inspired by the surrounding district that housed the lace market back in the day. We'll enter through the reception shop where you can find books, jewelry, and prints of some of the artwork. We'll have plenty of time to purchase items at the end of our day. Gallery Three is behind the shop, and Gallery One is to the right." He checked his wristwatch. "We have about thirty minutes before the next group comes through, so take your time."

He leaned against the doorway as the group separated into

pairs and trios to wander throughout the room. Leighanne broke away and walked to an abstract piece by Barbara Hepworth. She stood motionless and stared at the sculpture. What was she thinking? He used to be able to tell.

She turned, and the lights glinted off the chunky metal bracelet that encircled her wrist. A matching necklace hung around her neck. It glistened against her black sleeveless blouse, a stark contrast to the creamy white skin of her arms. Her sandaled feet poked out below hot pink slacks that came to her calf. Her toenails had been painted bright pink as well. Dressed to the nines as always, even though it was a casual outing.

Leighanne shuffled to the other side of the room and squatted in front of Eduardo Paolozzi's *The Frog*. Her finger hovered above the amphibian tracing the lines of his body.

Was she remembering something in particular? Wishing she was on her own cruise across the waters? What was it like to be Leighanne Webster? Crowds of people clamoring for autographs, seeing your name in neon lights high above the entrance to one of Broadway's famous theatres, cocktail parties...life with the "beautiful people."

He frowned. She could have it. Nottingham may not be New York City, but it had plenty to offer. And Lily was here. Lily. Her wan face came to mind, and his heart pricked. His brave Lily.

Always the strong one, even in her weakness.

Mentally shaking himself, he shifted from one foot to the other. He was getting maudlin. Pasting a smile on his face, he watched Leighanne rise and saunter to a series of paintings. A half-smile rested on her face as she gazed at the pictures.

A middle-aged man and woman joined Leighanne at the display. She gave them a brief nod and turned back to the oils. The couple did a double take and nudged each other. Apparently, they had recognized her. How did that happen? They weren't part of the production. How could they know who she was?

He stiffened, but remained against the wall. Had they sent the flowers? Were they stalking her? Heads close together, they whispered at length. When the woman nodded and reached into her purse, Jamison jerked upright and strode toward them then stopped as the woman's hand emerged clutching a small piece of paper and pen. Autograph seekers.

She held the scrap toward Leighanne, "Miss Webster, would you mind giving us your autograph? We saw you in *Hamlet* two years ago and thought you were wonderful. We had hoped to get back to New York, but..." The woman shrugged.

Leighanne pivoted toward them, and her face brightened. She reached for the paper and said, "Of course. To whom should I make it out?"

"Ethel and Warren Burger."

Leighanne bent and scribbled on the page before handing it back to the woman. Her companion held up a small digital camera. "Could we have your picture, too?"

Jamison continued toward them. "How about if I take the photo? That way you can both be in it."

The couple beamed at him, and the man handed him the device. They snuggled up against Leighanne, and he saw a momentary look of dismay cross her face before she gave them a cordial smile.

"On three. One...two...three." He pressed the button, and the shutter clicked. Rushing forward, he pressed the camera into the man's hands before guiding the two admirers toward the doorway of the gallery. "There is much more to see. Why don't you head to the next exhibit?"

Jamison turned and winked at Leighanne. "You were obliging to them. How do you do it?"

"What do you mean?"

"Cuddle up to perfect strangers for photo opportunities. Give autographs at the grocery store or wherever people happen to accost you."

She gave a dismissive wave. "It's not so bad. In fact, it's nice to be remembered, considering the condition of my bruised ego."

"I don't suppose it counts that I remember you."

Leighanne shook her head, and he sighed at the defeat on her face. Lord, wipe away her fears and discouragement. Help me know how to support her.

Be her friend.

Under his breath, Jamison said, "I can do that."

Confusion flitted across Leighanne's face. "What?"

"Uh...nothing." He held out his elbow. "Miss Webster, care to join me for today's final tour stop?"

She giggled and tucked her hand in the crook of his arm. "Certainly, Mr. Blake."

The softness of her fingers tingled on his skin, and he shot a final prayer heavenward. Just friends, Lord? I'm going to need your help here.

He led her forward, and they sauntered toward the next gallery.

Back at the rehearsal hall, Jamison clapped his hands then raised his voice to be heard over the chatter. "Listen up, people. The tour took a bit longer than anticipated, and we've got a lot of work to do to repair the costumes. Let's take a twenty-minute break then meet in the prop room."

Turning to Leighanne, he said, "No rest for the weary. I've got a surprise to show you. If you'll follow me..."

"What..."

He put a finger to her lips and grinned. "It wouldn't be a surprise if I told you. You hated secrets, even when we were little."

The pair pushed their way through the cast members and headed down the hallway. Their sandaled feet slapped on the floor as they hurried through the castle. A few moments later, they were in the prop room surrounded by wooden trees, racks of clothing and several rubber bins filled with arrows. Tom and his team must be working round the clock to replace the broken shafts.

Jamison led her to the ornate marble fireplace that filled the far wall. "Are you ready?"

"Ready for what? Are you going to build me a fire? Because I don't think that's going to work. There's no chimney."

He gaped at her, "How did you know that?"

"I didn't realize it until a few days ago. I was outside in the gardens and ended up on one of the benches. I found myself studying the house. I counted the chimneys then thought about the number of fireplaces. I reviewed the floor plan in my head, and that's when I figured out there's no chimney on the roof at this end of the building."

"You're amazing. I've worked here for five years and didn't figure it out until yesterday."

She blushed, and he smiled at her consternation. "Wait until you see this." He reached up and pressed one of the carved vases on the mantle. A grinding sound filled the room, and the back of the fireplace slid open.

Chapter Sixteen

Leighanne sat on the edge of the stage. Kelli and Jamison were in the back of the auditorium talking with the sound guy. He gestured wildly and punched the air with his hands as he spoke.

Her thoughts trailed back to Jamison's surprise in the prop room. He produced a flashlight and invited her to explore the passageway. All he needed was a fedora and a whip to be her Indiana Jones.

With only a few minutes until rehearsal, they picked their way through the recess behind the fireplace. The humid air enveloped them as Jamison's light bounced off the darkened walls. The stone floor was uneven and slick with dampness so she clung to his hand as he led her forward.

She followed him deeper into the castle and waited for her usual claustrophobia to overwhelm her, but it never happened. Any other time, she'd have been sweating like a pig and fighting for air. Instead, all she was aware of was peace—and Jamison's fingers laced with hers. They followed the tunnel for several yards and stumbled onto a half dozen boxes filled with the missing arrows. Who else knew about the passageway?

Kelli and Jamison joined the group near the platform, and Leighanne fought the urge to stare at him. This had to stop. As soon as the play was over, she was returning to New York to mend her tattered career. She couldn't do that from England. Surely one of her contacts would give her a chance at another production—something small perhaps.

Besides, Jamison's life was here. With Lily. And his castles.

Leighanne frowned. Lily seemed weaker during their last visit together, her ashen face even more pale than the last time she had seen Jamison's sister. But as always, Lily had managed to deflect the conversation away from herself and toward the Festival and upcoming performance. Because Leighanne wasn't family, the doctors wouldn't tell her anything. Maybe she could pry information from one of the nurses. It was bad, but how bad?

She raised her eyes toward the ceiling. Lord, touch Lily. You can heal her, whether through a miracle or through surgery. Don't let her die. That would devastate Jamison. He'd be alone.

He'd have you.

Heat rushed to her face at God's response, and she tossed a look over her shoulder. Had anyone else heard that? With an embarrassed laugh at herself, her gaze strayed to Jamison. He was staring at her with a bemused expression. When his eyes met hers, a smile spread across his face, and she looked away. Caught like a sixteen-year-old schoolgirl with a crush.

Kelli shouted, "Okay, everyone. We're finally ready to go through the scene with Robin, Marian and the sheriff. But don't go far, because the next one we're going to rehearse is at the marketplace, and that involves most of you."

Leighanne rose as Jamison ran up the aisle then leapt onto the stage. Several of the cast members applauded. Gordon Peters emerged from behind the curtain and smirked, "You know you could use the stairs like everyone else, Jamison."

"Just staying in character, Sheriff. You should try it."

"Vaulting onto the platform? No, thanks."

Jamison grinned, "I meant staying in character."

Gordon mugged a dark look and pointed at Jamison. "Arrest that man for foolishness!" He grinned, "How's that?"

Jamison seesawed his hand. "Not bad, but--"

The door at the back of the auditorium opened with a bang. A wiry teenager with long, dark hair entered. In his arms was a massive bouquet of red roses nestled amidst deep green ferns and white baby's breath. He ambled toward the stage. "Is there a Leighanne Webster here? These are for her."

From the corner of her eye Leighanne saw Jamison's face whip toward her. As she goggled at the huge floral arrangement, she lifted a tentative hand. "That's me."

The young man loped up the steps and onto the stage, Kelli close behind him. He pressed the flowers into her arms then held out a clipboard. "Sign on the last line, please."

Leighanne struggled to balance the flowers while trying to catch the pen that danced on the end of the chain attached to the clipboard. Gordon held out his hand. "I'll sign for you, Leighanne. No need to drop those."

The heavy fragrance from the blooms filled her nose as she nodded. "Thanks."

After signing his name with a flourish, Gordon dug into his pocket then thrust some cash into the teen's hand. "Thank you, young man."

The boy looked at the bills and grinned as he pocketed the money. "Thanks, governor." He sauntered off the stage and down the aisle toward the door.

Leighanne said, "I can pay you back, Gordon."

"Nonsense." He dug an elbow into Jamison's side. "Way to go, Jamie."

Jamison's face darkened. "They're not from me."

"Well, if you didn't send them, who did?"

"We'd all like to know."

Kelli rushed forward and poked a finger into the flowers. "Is there a card? Surely there's a card."

Leighanne shook her head. "Just like the last ones."

Her sister turned toward the people seated in the auditorium. "Did any of you send these?"

Leighanne waited, her eyes darting from one face to the next. Had one of the cast members sent these? All were shaking their heads. Was someone lying?

She refused to look at Jamison although she could sense his stare. Why was he so mad? It was just flowers.

Kelli pivoted toward Leighanne and Jamison. "Guess we've still got a mystery on our hands."

Jamison said, "I find it hard to believe you don't know who sent these. Did you leave a boyfriend in New York? Maybe you sent them to yourself."

A frown creased Kelli's forehead. "Why would she do that?"

"I don't know. To make me jealous? To put the shine back on her reputation?"

Tears welled up in Leighanne's eyes, and she blinked to keep them from spilling over. Why did she cry when she got mad? She spoke past the lump in her throat. "To make you jealous? Jealous of what? A career in shambles? A solitary life with no close friends?"

She buried her face in the flowers for a moment then glared at him. "You obviously don't know me like you thought, Jamison Blake. Of course you didn't send these. How could you? You're not capable of anything as nice as a bouquet of flowers."

The door in the back of the auditorium opened with another bang.

"Darling! I see you got my flowers!"

As one, everyone in the room turned toward the burly man in expensive Italian shoes striding down the aisle toward the platform. Dressed in a black leather trench coat with a red silk scarf draped under the collar, he was straight out of the pages of *GQ*. The unbuttoned coat revealed a charcoal gray double-breasted suit, light blue shirt and multi-colored tie that looked like an impressionist painting. His overly long blond hair was swept back and tied into a ponytail.

Leighanne fisted her hands and folded her arms. What was he doing here? How did he find her? She hadn't told anyone where she was going.

Jamison and Kelli were frozen in place, eyes riveted on the guy who marched up the stairs and across the stage. He enveloped Leighanne into a hug then stepped back and made a show of examining her.

He stroked his jaw in an exaggerated motion. "Why haven't you said anything? Have you missed me? I've certainly missed you.

That's why all the flowers. I can't believe you up and left me. Left the production and New York. How did you get caught up in an amateur production like this?"

When he moved forward as if to hug her again, Leighanne held out her arms to block him. Her mouth worked awkwardly as she decided which question to ask first. She finally spit out, "What are you doing here?"

"I told you! I missed you! Now, are you going to answer my questions?"

Kelli cleared her throat and gave her a wide-eyed stare. Leighanne sprang forward. "Uh, I'm sorry. Let me introduce you. This is my sister Kelli Norcott, and my...uh...friend Jamison Blake. The rest of the folks are my cast and crew. Everyone, this is Preston Bedrosian. He was the director of my last production."

Jamison's face was stiff as he dipped his head in a curt nod. Kelli held out her hand, and the man grasped it gently and raised it to his lips. "A pleasure to meet you, Ms. Norcott."

Kelli colored. Preston released her hand and bowed to the troupe. He straightened and turned to Leighanne. "I'm here to take you to dinner. We must discuss our future together."

Leighanne narrowed her eyes. "I can't go to dinner with you. I'm in the middle of rehearsal, Preston."

He waved his hand. "Pish-posh. They can do without you for a few hours. We must go now. I'm on the next flight out."

"You can't just sashay in here and expect me to fall at your feet." Leighanne's voice was hard, "Did you forget that you fired me?"

"All a misunderstanding. You must come with me. I can't live without you."

"Don't be melodramatic, Preston."

Jamison walked to the edge of the platform and faced the crowd. "We're done for tonight, folks. See you Thursday." Without a backward glance, he stalked offstage, his heels sharp against the wooden floor.

Chapter Seventeen

Jamison slumped in the hard plastic chair next to the hospital bed. His arms lay lifeless in his lap. "Why did I think she could still love me, Lily?"

His sister reached over from the bed and stroked his arm. "She does love you, Jamie. She may not realize it, but she does."

"How can you say that?"

"Why do you think she came back to England?"

He sat up. "To help Kelli with the play."

Lily shook her head. "She needs to heal. And what better place to do it than back here with those who love her most? She knew she'd see you. We've been friends with the Websters since we were kids. Even if she didn't know you were involved in the play, deep down she knew you were still in Kelli's life."

"That's a leap in logic, sis."

She shrugged, "Think what you want, but I'm sure she still loves you."

"How can I compete with New York?" He sat up and ran his

hands through his hair. "You should have seen the guy. Thousand dollar suit and Italian loafers. Manicured fingers. And he was her director. He can make her a star."

"Key word: was."

"What?"

"He *was* her director. She left him, remember."

"I think he's more than her director. He said something about wanting to discuss their future together. Apparently, he wants to marry her."

Lily gripped his arm, and he looked up to find her glaring at him. "Wow, that's a dark look."

"Well, you can be so obtuse sometimes. You ever think he might want to discuss their future professional lives. After all, he was her director."

"He called her 'darling' and sent her four massive, high-priced bouquets. Does that sound like a director-actor relationship?"

She sat back against her pillows and crossed her arms. "Yes. That's the way those people are. Calling each other by endearments. Kissing for no reason. Don't you watch the movies?"

"Actually, no."

"You should."

He grinned at her. "Yeah, that's where I want to learn about 'real life.'"

She stuck out her tongue then smiled in return. "Okay, so maybe what happens in the movies isn't realistic, but I'm sticking by my opinion. I think Leighanne still loves you. And it's up to you to help her see that."

Jamison shifted toward Lily and grimaced. "Could they make these chairs any more uncomfortable?"

She patted the bed. "Sit over here."

"That's okay." He glanced at his watch. "I can't stay much longer."

"Are you avoiding the conversation?"

Huffing a deep sigh, he shrugged, "Probably. But seriously, Lily, even if I do make her admit her feelings for me, we could never have a relationship. Her work is in New York, and mine is here."

"Does it have to be? You know, there are more than just a few museums in New York. I'm pretty sure you could get a job."

"We'd never see each other. She works nights, and I'd work days. That's not a relationship. That's being roommates."

She slashed the air with her hand. "Logistics. Don't lose her again because of logistics. Daddy traveled all the time, and mom sometimes went with him. That was how they worked it out. If you two want to be together, you can figure something out."

"Then we're back to square one. What's to say she wants to be with me?"

"The way her voice softens when she says your name. Or the fact that she blushes every time someone else says your name."

He gaped at her. "She does that?"

A smug smile blossomed on her face. "Yes. Several times when she was here for a visit. Trust me on this, Jamie. And pray about it. God will help you find a way to make this work."

Jamison sagged back into the chair. "I'm not so sure about that, sis. I'm thinking of finishing the play like I promised Kelli then going somewhere else for a fresh start. Maybe I'll go back to London. There are plenty of museums in the city."

"What is going on with you? I've never seen you give up like this."

"I'm not giving up. I'm facing reality. Leighanne loves someone else, and her life is in New York."

Kelli entered the room. "I wouldn't be so sure about that."

Chapter Eighteen

Leighanne scanned the restaurant. Small tables covered in white cloths topped with flickering candles and gleaming utensils were placed strategically around the room – close enough to feel cozy yet spaced enough to afford privacy. Tuxedo clad wait staff hovered at discrete distances springing to action at the slightest indication from a patron.

Her exquisitely prepared coq au vin grew cold as she pushed the food around on her plate. She allowed Preston to bully her into dinner with him, and he had selected one of the most expensive restaurants in Nottingham, of course. She'd rather be sitting cross-legged on the floor at Kelli's coffee table sharing a pile of fish and chips wrapped in butcher paper.

"Not to your liking, Leighanne? You could order something else." Preston raised his arm, and their server rushed to his side.

The man bowed. "Yes, sir?"

"We'd like to see the menu again."

"Preston, no." She speared a piece of the chicken and smiled at the waiter. "I'm fine. Thank you."

"Are you sure, miss?"

"Absolutely." She poked the food into her mouth and made a show of chewing with pleasure. She swallowed and poked another piece into her mouth. It was going to be a long meal.

Preston waved his hand, dismissing the server. The man bowed and moved away. Leighanne laid down her fork and reached for her goblet at the same time Preston reached for her hand. Their fingers collided with the glass, and it wobbled wildly. They both grabbed for it and met empty air as the crystal chalice tumbled onto its side with a thud. The tablecloth absorbed the sparkling water as their server hurried back with a busboy carrying a tray.

With practiced grace, the waiter plucked the glass, salt and pepper shakers, and bread plates from the table and put them on the tray. The busboy scuttled back to the kitchen and disappeared through the doors. Meanwhile, their server whipped a linen napkin from his back pocket and sopped up the moisture.

Leighanne stammered an apology.

The waiter shook his head. "No problem, miss. We'll have you fixed up in a jiffy." Another server arrived with fresh tableware, and the two quickly set the items on the table. "Will there be anything else, sir? Miss?"

Preston gestured toward Leighanne's food. "I think Ms. Webster is finished. Isn't that right, Leighanne?"

"The meal was lovely. I don't have much of an appetite this evening."

"Very good, miss." The man whisked their plates away, hers still ladened with food, Preston's clean except for a few crumbs.

Silence descended over the table while Leighanne fiddled with the remaining silverware.

"Being in England suits you."

Preston wore a perplexed expression. He pushed his chair back from the table, crossed his long legs, and cradled his water glass in one hand. The candles' flames flickered on the lenses of his rimless eyeglasses. His blue-black hair was spiked in the latest trendy look.

"Preston, why are you here?"

He took a sip of water. "I already told you. I want you in my next production. You'd be perfect for the lead. Especially now."

"Isn't that a little risky for you, considering my last part ended in disaster?"

Shaking his head, he set the goblet on the table then steepled his fingers. "I don't think so. You've changed since I last saw you. You've got more confidence, more...something...something I can't quite figure out. What have you been doing?"

"Doing? Nothing. Well, helping my sister with the annual play for the Robin Hood Festival. You know, coaching the cast members, painting the scenery, stuff like that."

"And playing Maid Marian."

Leighanne bolted upright in the chair. "How do you know that?"

"Your sponsor has been busy sending out press releases. We got one at the theatre."

"The theatre? The one in New York? Why would he do that?"

Preston rubbed his jaw. "Don't you get it? You're a commodity. It's a feather in his cap to have you associated with this production. He wants everyone to know about it – especially those of us on Broadway."

Leighanne licked her dry lips then took a deep drink of water. She set down the glass with a muted thud and rubbed the goblet's stem. "So it should prove to be a media circus."

He shrugged. "It's a good possibility. But I'm not here to talk about that." Reaching inside his jacket pocket, he pulled out a folded sheaf of papers. He laid it on the table between them then drew her hand into his. Running a finger down her arm, he said, "I'm dead serious about working with you again. You're a brilliant actress who's had a bit of a setback—nothing that can't be reversed. Take your time, but think about it. That's all I ask."

The skin on her arm crawled where it contacted his. Could she work with him again? Could she go back on stage in New York? Did she want to? She froze. Where had that thought come from? Of course she wanted to be on Broadway. It was her life's dream. At least it had been.

Preston withdrew his hand. "Will you promise me to think about it? Just because you don't want to marry me doesn't mean we can't be partners on the stage."

"Listen, Preston. About that...I realize I hurt your feelings when I said no and broke up with you. It was inexcusable, and I'm sorry."

"See? That's what I mean about you being different. Apologizing. Which, by the way, you don't have to. I'm the one who should be begging for forgiveness. I was a jerk." He ducked his head. "I didn't exactly treat you as you deserved."

She gave him a tender smile. "Now, who's different?"

"Seriously, can you forgive me?"

"Already done. We weren't ready to have a relationship in the glare of the media."

"Perhaps, but that didn't excuse my behavior. What about now? Could we try again?" He narrowed his eyes at her. "Or is there someone else? Perhaps young Mr. Blake who stormed from the auditorium?"

Heat suffused her face. She shifted in her seat, fiddling with her napkin. "No. We were engaged a long time ago. There's nothing now. It could never be."

His eyes twinkled. "If you're trying to convince me, you'll have to do a better acting job."

Her hands stilled. "I'd rather not discuss it."

He held up his hands in surrender. "No problem. Why don't you tell me about this production? What's it like working with amateurs again? Must be unbearable."

Leighanne took a sip from her water glass. "Many of them are quite proficient. And they're good sports. Everyone is pitching in. We've had some setbacks with props and costumes, and the folks are working extra hours so we'll be ready for the first night. A lot of them have been involved in this thing for years. They can probably quote the lines in their sleep."

She folded her arms. "They may not be receiving money, but they act like professionals. Nothing is too much trouble. It's all about the production—a refreshing change from New York where it's all about the performers and what's in it for them. When's the last time you were in a production where there were no prima donnas?"

He shook his head. "I can't remember."

"My point exactly."

He leaned forward. "Don't you miss it? Even a little?"

She took another swallow from her water glass and blew out a breath.

A frown wrinkled his forehead. "What?"

"You're going to think it's foolish. You'll laugh at me."

"Darling, I would never make fun of you. You may not love me, but I care for you. Why else would I come almost four thousand miles to see you?"

"To talk me into playing your lead. You must not be able to find anyone else."

Preston grasped his chest. "You're killing me."

Leighanne giggled. He was a good man despite his oversized ego and need for constant adulation. "Okay, I'll tell you." She took a deep breath and began, "I'm performing for an audience of one."

"Who...?"

She laid a finger on his lips for a moment. "Let me finish."

He grinned and gestured for her to continue.

Leighanne straightened and stared into his eyes. "I'm performing for my Lord now—not a roomful of people. God has given me this talent, and I need to use it for Him, for His glory. I've realized it's all about Him, not me. He needs me here. I'm not being paid to perform, but if I do, the man who is backing the production will pay for a very costly operation for a friend of mine. Saying it like that makes it sound bad, but it isn't. I'm even getting past the panic attacks. I've still got a long way to go, but God is healing me. Does any of this make sense to you?"

He shook his head. "Not really. The God I was exposed to, as a child, was heavy-handed and spiteful. My parents used him as an excuse to belittle and abuse my brother and me."

Her hands fluttered to her throat. "How awful for you! But that wasn't God. It was your parents. God loves you."

"He has a funny way of showing it. Why didn't He protect us?"

Tears filled her eyes, and she dabbed at them. "I don't know. God's ways are mysterious. That sounds like a platitude, but it's the truth. He's the creator, and we're His creation. We can't be expected to understand everything. It's where faith comes in."

She fell quiet as their waiter approached the table. "Will there be anything else, sir? Dessert perhaps?"

Preston looked at her with a raised eyebrow. "Sweets for the sweet?"

Leighanne shook her head, and he turned to the server. "Just the check, please."

"Very good, sir." He walked away on silent feet, and they were alone again.

Preston stared at her. "You're serious about this, aren't you?"

"Yes. I wish you could know God like I do."

"Perhaps if you came to New York, you could teach me."

"You can find Him without me. The Bible says, 'I love those who love me; and those who diligently seek me will find me.'" She reached into her purse and pulled out a small, leather-bound volume and laid it on the table. "It's all in here. Start with Luke. He wanted to know about Jesus, too, so he interviewed a bunch of people. I don't know if he was a skeptic to start with or had heard the stories and wanted proof. But he found it. And you can, too."

He tapped the roll of papers between them. "If you'll consider coming back to New York, I'll read this Luke guy."

She picked up the papers and slid them into her pocketbook. "I don't like making this kind of a deal, but if that's what it takes, so be it. Promise me you'll read with an open mind."

Preston tucked the Bible into the breast pocket of his jacket. "I promise. But you must do the same. Truly consider the contract."

Her heart thumped unevenly. What had she gotten herself into?

Chapter Nineteen

The auditorium door opened with a squeal. At the noise, Jamison nearly fell from the ladder where he stood hanging the last of the lights. He swallowed his irritation and turned toward the sound. His breath caught. Leighanne trotted down the aisle toward him.

She wore bright yellow pants and an oversized white button-down shirt. Strappy brown sandals were on her slender feet. Even dressed casually, she was beautiful enough to walk a runway. Her face shone. Apparently, she had already forgotten their argument. Or maybe she didn't care.

As she approached, he scrambled down the rungs to the floor. He shoved his fisted hands into his pockets and waited. Smiling, she jogged up the side stairs and onto the stage. He tried not to glower when she came to a stop in front of him.

Her smile faltered, and her arms fell to her sides, dangling lifelessly. Her eyes looked everywhere except at him. "Jamison, you'll never believe it. I've been offered a part in another Broadway production. They still want me...well...at least Preston does. Isn't that wonderful? I thought my career was over, that they'd never take me back. And I owe it all to you. I wanted to thank you."

"Me? What did I do?"

"You helped me regain my confidence. Can't you see that?"

He pulled his hands from his pockets and crossed his arms. "I did nothing of the sort. It was the Lord, Leighanne. He healed you. I simply prayed for you."

His voice, monotone and clinical, echoed in the empty room. She was leaving again. Lily was right, and he had ignored all her warnings. He should be prepared for Leighanne's departure. But no, he had clung to a thread of hope that she might still care for him, enough to want to stay in England. He was a fool, but at least Lily wouldn't be an I-told-you-so.

Leighanne's shoulders drooped, and her feet shuffled. The air seemed to go out of her excitement. "This is a big opportunity, Jamison. I can prove I've still got what it takes. If I don't accept this role, I might never get another chance. Broadway directors and producers have long memories. One flop, and you're branded a failure. I can't afford to let that happen."

He shrugged. "You need to do what's right for you. Are you leaving right away?"

She shook her head. "No. I've committed to playing Marian. I wouldn't walk out on you. What do you take me for?"

"A professional actress. You can't let our pathetic little festival get in your way. I understand. I'm sure I can find someone to take your place."

"But..."

Jamison strode back to the ladder. He bent to retrieve the end of the string of lights. He hesitated and wheeled back toward Leighanne. "Listen, Leighanne. I understand you need to go. Your career is important to you. I get that. We've managed quite nicely without you in the past. Go back to New York."

Emotions fought for supremacy on her face. And if he didn't know better, love—or at least the vestiges of it—mixed with anxiety, regret and disappointment.

Leighanne bowed her head for a long moment. The silence hung like a shroud between them. He couldn't tear his eyes away. He watched and waited. The light glistened off her hair, and her lips moved, yet he couldn't hear her. Was she praying, or arguing with herself?

She finally raised her eyes to his. When she spoke her voice was barely above a whisper. "I know I've hurt you—too often to count. I'm sorry for making assumptions about the flowers. Can you ever forgive me?"

"There's nothing to forgive."

Taking a step closer, she reached toward him. He caught a light floral scent and flinched. Her arms dropped to her side.

Nothing like the aroma of her perfume to take him back to old times. Sitting in Hyde Park with a picnic lunch, packed into one of the crowded cars on the Eye, snuggling in front of her fireplace as flames danced in the dim room.

A couple of years ago, while on the Tube, he smelled the scent. He couldn't remember what it was called, but he'd know it anywhere. He searched the car for several minutes before berating himself for his foolishness.

Lord, help me let her go again. You know what's best for her, for us. She needs her career, and I need to be here for Lily. It's not going to work. I just need you to dull the pain.

I know the plans I have for you...plans to prosper you and not to harm you, plans to give you a hope and a future. Seriously, Lord?

Confusion crossed Leighanne's face. She must think he'd lost his mind, staring at her without saying a word. He cleared his throat and tried to ignore the hollowness in his heart.

"It's okay if you go, Leighanne. I understand. Like you said, if you don't take this, you might not get another chance. Don't worry about the argument. We've been bickering since we were kids. What's another misunderstanding? I'm thrilled you have this opportunity. You're a wonderful actress. The stage shouldn't lose you."

She nibbled her lower lip and seemed to study him. "I won't leave you in a bind. I told Preston I would finish my commitment, and I meant it. You're very generous to offer to let me out of it."

Could he work with her knowing she was going to be gone again? He'd have to.

Chapter Twenty

The children's giggles mingled with the roar of traffic as Leighanne and Kelli walked them home from school. Charlotte hopped over the seams of the sidewalk, her backpack swinging like a pendulum with each step, and her singsong voice squeaking out nursery rhymes. Edmund sauntered alongside them, periodically crouching to inspect a miniscule treasure such as a bug or stone.

Parents and youngsters surged around them in the sunshine, waving and calling farewells when they broke off at intersections. The crowd grew sparse, and after twenty minutes the foursome was alone. They turned onto Waverly Street and approached the entrance to the Arboretum.

Charlotte tugged on Kelli's arm. "Mummy, it's so pretty out. May we go to the park?"

Kelli said, "How much homework do you have?"

"Some math problems and my spelling words. It shouldn't take me too long."

Kelli raised an eyebrow at her daughter. "Are you sure, or are you telling me that so I'll say yes?"

"I can show you, if you like."

Kelli turned to Leighanne. "Do you mind? She's right; it's a beautiful day."

Leighanne shook her head. "Not at all."

Smiling, Kelli gestured toward the park. "You talked us into it. We can stay for about forty-five minutes."

The kids cheered and raced ahead, their feet slapping against the pavement. Leighanne and Kelli ambled behind them. The children slid off their packs and propped them underneath a nearby bench before galloping onto the grass. Leighanne grinned as they somersaulted and tumbled on the knoll. Oh, to have half that amount of energy!

The women sat down with a sigh, their backs to the pond and the sun. Birds called to them from the aviary a short distance away. Leighanne pushed her arms into the air in a luxurious stretch. Her spine crackled and popped with the movement, and Kelli gave her a sideways glance. Leighanne retrieved her cell phone from her purse and snapped several shots of the youngsters' antics before tucking the device into her pocket.

A gray-haired couple strolled past with clasped hands. The man bent his head toward the woman who talked to him in a low voice. At least eighty years old, they seemed oblivious to their surroundings. Leighanne studied them. What would it be like to know someone for fifty years or more? To love them for that long? It hardly seemed possible in this day and age.

Jamison's face sprang to her mind, and she warmed. She shook her head to rid herself of the vision and focused on the children. Sensing Kelli's stare, she turned and looked at her sister. "What?"

"I don't know. You seem restless. What's going on?"

"You always could read me like a book."

Kelli's eyes sparkled. "As any good sister should."

"Exactly. You're the good sister."

Sputtering Kelli sat up straighter. "Hey. That's not what I meant."

Leighanne chortled, "Gotcha!"

Kelli nudged her shoulder then crossed her arms. "Okay, so now that you've tried to divert my attention, are you going to tell me what you're thinking about?"

Leighanne shrugged, and they sat in silence for several minutes. Did she want to talk about the tug of war inside herself? She had the opportunity to resurrect her career, yet all she could think about was Jamison Blake, mooning over him like a teenager. She had a life in New York she had worked hard to build. What would her colleagues say? Did it matter? Why was she thinking about making a change? He wasn't interested. He told her to leave.

She ran a hand through her hair, lifting the heavy curls from her shoulders. A breeze tickled her neck, and she dropped the tresses.

Kelli scooted closer. "It doesn't take a rocket scientist to see that you and Jamison still have feelings for each other. But the stage is calling your name. You want to stay, but at the same time you want to go."

Leighanne hunched over her legs, her arms dangling between her knees.

"Have you prayed about the situation?" Kelli's voice was urgent.

Did the comments and complaints she hurled at God count as prayer? Blitzing him with her dictums? Her face fell. Probably not.

Leighanne didn't look at Kelli as she spoke. "First of all, you're wrong about Jamison. He doesn't care about me. He as much as told me this morning when he said I should leave, to take the new part."

"I disagree. I think he's telling you what he thinks you want to hear. He doesn't want to hold you back. You two are repeating what happened five years ago. Having said that, in the event you are right, then you shouldn't be having any conflict."

Leighanne blew several stray strands from her eyes. "I know! That's what's so weird. This decision should be a no-brainer. But every time I think about signing on the dotted line, I feel like I'm doing something wrong. How can that be?"

"What if it's God? You didn't tell me whether you've prayed about this, but if you have, maybe this is his answer."

"How can *not* accepting this contract possibly be what I'm supposed to do?"

Charlotte raced toward them, a clump of dandelions clutched in one hand. "Mummy! Auntie Leighanne! Look what I found for you."

She held out the bedraggled flowers, and Kelli took the bouquet, her face wreathed in smiles. She enveloped Charlotte in a hug. "They're gorgeous, honey. You're very sweet to bring them to us."

"Mama, can you and Aunt Leighanne play Blind Man's Bluff with us?"

Laying the blossoms in her lap, she wiped her hands on her jeans. "Certainly." She rose and pulled Leighanne to her feet as Charlotte wheeled around and sprinted back toward her brother.

Kelli linked her arm with Leighanne's. "You know as well as I do that we can't see the big picture God has for us. We need to trust Him and take it one day at a time. Hard as it may be to believe, He may have something different for you in mind."

"But I love the theatre."

"Yes, and I doubt He'd take that away from you, but if you follow His leading, He may give you something you love even more than performing."

A frown pulled at Leighanne's lips. "I can't imagine."

"And I never thought I would be working in a castle, raising two kids and producing a play."

"What makes you think Jamison still loves me? He told me to go, that he would fill the role if I left before opening night – which I told him I wouldn't do."

"He wants you to have what you want, even if it means he has to step aside to grant your wish. It's what he did five years ago, and he's apparently willing to do it again. He would do anything for you. It's what people do for those they love. Haven't you noticed? His face lights up when you enter a room. Actually, it lights up even if you're not there, but if your name is mentioned. He follows your every move, aware of your location at any time."

Leighanne glanced at Kelli. "You're making that up."

Kelli's gaze bore into hers. "No, I'm not. Next time we're at rehearsal, check it out. See for yourself. Put off that director guy. Tell him you need another week to decide."

"That wouldn't be fair. He needs time to find someone if I don't take the part."

"If he's the professional you say he is, he'll give you the time.

He sprang this on you. He certainly can't expect a decision overnight."

Leighanne rubbed her jaw. "Yes, he can. Any actress on Broadway would kill to work with Preston. You don't tell him no."

Her sister narrowed her eyes. Leighanne tried not to squirm under her scrutiny. Kelli smoothed her blouse down over her slacks as they reached the children. "We'll finish this later. Now, for a little fun."

Kelli pulled the scarf from around her neck and dangled it in the air. "Who wants to be blind first?"

Charlotte and Edmund squealed and pointed to Leighanne. "Auntie Leighanne! Auntie Leighanne!"

Kelli looked at Leighanne and raised her eyebrows in question.

Leighanne shrugged. "Why not?" She turned her back to her sister who wrapped the gauzy fabric around her eyes and tied it snugly behind her head. She could hear the kids running and jumping around her. Giggling, they poked her then dashed away as she stumbled through the grass.

Despite the gaiety of the children, her thoughts darkened. Why did life have to be so complicated? She never should have returned to England. Somebody once said you can never go back. She was beginning to see the truth in the statement. She should have stayed in New York, no matter how bad things had been. Too late now.

The wind picked up, and Leighanne shivered. She took Kelli's advice and stopped in her tracks. "Lord, I don't know what to do. You've given me the gift of acting. I'm supposed to use it, right? Where else can I use my talents but New York? Jamison told me to go. Is Kelli right? Does he still love me? He's simply being nice, isn't he?"

Her voice stilled, and she waited. And waited. Nothing.

Now, what?

Chapter Twenty-One

The following evening members of the stage crew discussed the logistics of changing the props in the current scene with the next one. Cast and seamstresses chattered about the costumes as last minute adjustments were made. At the far end of the platform, Leighanne stood statue-like as Renee, one of the production assistants, struggled to pin some sort of head covering on her.

Jamison watched the pair. Obviously nervous, Renee dropped the hat several times before finally attaching it to Leighanne's hair, and her face and neck were mottled with red blotches. Leighanne gave her a gentle smile then said something that caused them both to giggle.

Jamison looked down and paged through his script, making notations in the margins about a few places in the cast's performance that needed to be smoothed out. Footsteps approached, and he looked up.

Clutching several newspapers and a large roll of paper, Kelli strode toward him. Two weeks remained until the first performance, and she was starting to get uptight about the publicity. She had been badgering him for two days to do an interview with one of the local rags, and he just couldn't bring himself to care.

In a fortnight, it would all be over. Leighanne would be gone, and he could get on with his life. Ticket sales were going well. All three performances should sell out. Mr. Tillinghast would be happy then Lily could get her surgery. He scrubbed at his face. It was going to be a long fourteen days.

Kelli bobbled the papers in her arms, and he caught the roll as it launched itself from her hand. It unfurled, and Leighanne stared at him from the poster. His breath caught. It was Leighanne, but at the same time it wasn't her. She was Maid Marian – feminine, yet no shrinking violet. A woman to be reckoned with.

"She's quite good, isn't she?"

Unable to tear his eyes from the poster, Jamison nodded. "She's got the gift."

Kelli laid her hand on his arm. "You need to tell her how you feel, Jamison."

He looked from the poster to the actress. A crowd had gathered around Leighanne. Her face glowed, and he could hear bits and pieces of the conversation. The group was discussing her upcoming departure. Turning back to Kelli, he shook his head.

"No. She's made her decision. I'm not going to beg her to stay. I need to let her go. Forever."

Kelli chewed her lower lip, and her eyes welled with tears. He pulled the newspapers from her arms and laid them out on the music stand in front of them. "You're here about the interview, right? I'll do it. Set it up for tomorrow. The sooner we get it in the paper, the better."

Taking a swipe at her eyes, Kelli spoke through clenched teeth, "It boggles the mind how dense the two of you are. God has given you guys a second chance, and you're both walking away."

With that Kelli snatched the papers from the stand, whirled on her heel, and marched down the aisle toward the door. He didn't like upsetting her. She had been a friend through thick and thin – his parents' death, Lily's illness, the break up with Leighanne. Leighanne!

He tossed a glance over his shoulder and found Leighanne staring at him, anger darkening her face. She had apparently seen the altercation with her sister. Now, they were both angry at him. He dropped his eyes and turned back to the script. Nothing he could do about it. He sensed the daggers she shot his way, having been on the receiving end of it many times in the old days.

The poster lay on the floor where it had fallen. He picked it up and unrolled it. Once more Leighanne/Maid Marian gazed at him from the paper. The artist was very talented – intricate details created a photographic-like scene. He stroked the silky-looking hair that framed Leighanne's face.

He bowed his head. "Lord, I'm struggling here. I still love her. But I'm a simple man. I don't like crowds. I need open spaces. Leighanne is an important actress. I don't have anything to offer her. A marriage between us could never work. I need to let her go, but I didn't know it would hurt so badly. How can it be so painful to do what is right?"

Love her, my son.

"I do."

Just love her.

"I don't understand, Lord. I've told you I love her. Why do you keep saying that?"

Silence.

Jamison clenched his hands together. What did it all mean? He did love her. Was God telling him not to let her go? Was he telling him it would all work out? "God, what are you saying?"

Trust in me with all your heart, and lean not on your own understanding; in all your ways acknowledge me, and I will make your paths straight.

He was doing it again. Running ahead of the Lord and expecting him to keep pace. "Lord, forgive me. Forgive my disobedience and unbelief. I get it now. I will follow your commandment to love her. We'll figure the rest out as we go, won't we?"

Peace settled on him like a warm blanket, and he smiled. Opening his eyes, he wiped his hands on his jeans and rotated his shoulders.

The chattering swelled around him. A half-dozen women hovered around Leighanne, giggling and talking. He strained to hear them.

"...leave for New York?"

"As soon...play is over."

"You...be excited."

Leighanne's face brightened. "Absolutely."

Jamison clapped his hands, and the buzz of conversation ebbed away. The cast and crew turned toward him, expectancy on their faces. "Listen up, people. We're in the home stretch. You've done an incredible job of learning your lines and creating the props." A frown twisted his features. "And repairing the props. Ticket sales are strong, and we have Leighanne to thank for it."

A smattering of applause broke out, and Leighanne blushed. Jamison waited for it to cease before continuing. "As you all know, Ms. Webster has been offered an important role in an upcoming Broadway production. She'll leave us immediately after our last performance in order to begin rehearsals. And we *all* know how important rehearsals are, don't we?"

Laughter rolled through the auditorium, and he smiled in response. Winking at Leighanne, whose blush deepened, he said, "As much as we'd like to hear all about Ms. Webster's new adventure, there are a couple of scenes of our own we need to polish."

He skimmed the script until he came to the first set of notations. "I need Maid Marian and Friar Tuck. We'll be working on the third scene in the second act." His gaze swept the room. "Don't go far if you're Robin's men; we'll do the fifth scene after this."

Feet rumbled on the platform as the cast moved away – some to the chairs in the audience, others into the wings. The crew hastened to move the appropriate props into place. Jamison stood, arms crossed as the stage was transformed into Sherwood Forest.

He would miss working with these folks. They had knocked themselves out to get things ready. Not one complained about the long hours, and most had full-time jobs and families. He didn't need to tell them he wasn't returning. That would distract them. Maybe he'd say something when it was all over. Or not.

Chapter Twenty-Two

Leighanne studied herself in the full-length mirror back stage. The dark green dress fell in gentle folds to the floor, and brown half boots peeped out from underneath. Narrow sleeves hugged her arms, but did not restrict her movement. An ivory-colored sash wrapped snugly around her waist. A wreath of flowers encircled her hair that had been woven in a single braid. She turned one way then the other and smiled. A New York costuming department couldn't have done any better.

Dress rehearsal was over, and she needed to change back into her street clothes, but as was her habit in New York, she mulled over her performance before doing so. It helped to remain by herself in character. The others were jammed into the dressing rooms jabbering and shedding their costumes and their roles.

She smoothed the skirt and adjusted the belt, pondering the scenes one by one. Other than her miscue in the second scene of the first act, she had done well. No panic attacks. God had been with her the whole time. She had come a long way in eight weeks.

It had been a whirlwind, but nothing she couldn't handle.

She mugged at herself in the glass. Correction: nothing God couldn't handle. She prayed Jamison would join her in New York. The familiar pang struck her at the thought. She would miss working with these people, but she had nothing left in England. Jamison had made that clear.

Kelli thawed once Leighanne convinced her she was seriously considering God's will, but that didn't mean she was happy with the decision. She had extracted a promise that Leighanne would schedule regular trips back to the UK even if she were lucky enough for a long run on the play.

Leighanne uncinched the sash from her waist and took a deep breath enjoying the freedom of her loosened clothing. She removed the bobby pins that held the flowers in her hair. How had the real Maid Marian kept the wreath anchored? Had she worn one? Depending on whose research was used, Marian was a noblewoman. How had she made the decision to leave everything behind to follow Robin? Had it been worth it?

Muffled bangs filled the air as the stage crew prepared the set for tomorrow's performance. Despite the fact that they had to be exhausted, they were here before she arrived and long after she left. They were courteous, helpful and full of humor. Every one of them was a prankster at some level.

She chuckled at the memory of the parrots they hung in Sherwood Forest for tonight's rehearsal. There were dozens of the colorful birds, dangling from nearly every branch. The guys had gone about their business straight-faced and stoic as if nothing were amiss, even after the cast was helpless with laughter. Not one of them would let it slip as to who had come up with the idea.

Tom Haddonfield appeared behind her in the mirror. Their eyes met, and they both chuckled. Apparently he was remembering the parrots, too. She turned to greet him, and he made an exaggerated bow. "Maid Marian, you must be tired. How may I be of service to you?"

She plunked the flowers back on her head and draped the sash around her neck before performing an awkward curtsy. "I am a wee bit peckish, my lord, but not in need of anything. Thank you for your kind offer."

His blue eyes crinkled at the corners as he grinned. "You gave a great performance, Leighanne. I know I speak for the entire group when I say thanks for helping us out. You've been a gem to work with."

"It's been a wonderful experience, even with the stress of the broken props. Everyone has been friendly and welcoming. I won't forget it."

"I guess it's different in New York. What with money on the

line – that sort of thing."

Leighanne gave him a mock shiver. "You have no idea. Everyone is out for himself. You have to constantly prove yourself so you can get the next gig. Reputation is everything, and it doesn't take much to ruin it. There can be a lot of backbiting, and rumors run rampant."

Tom's forehead wrinkled. "Why would anyone work in that environment?"

"Some days, I ask myself the same question."

———————— ◆ ————————

The dressing room was empty. The cast was gone, and Leighanne sat on the couch, her eyes closed and her head resting against the lumpy cushion. Now in a T-shirt and jeans, she needed to put on her shoes and get home, but as always the solitude of the room cocooned her like no other place. What was it about a dressing room?

She sat up and rubbed at her eyes. She was too introspective tonight. She should go home and rest. Kelli tried to understand her need to stay for a while but had finally taken her leave an hour before, confusion on her face.

Bending over, Leighanne pulled her sneakers onto her feet and tied the laces. She wiggled her toes inside the constricting shoes then rose. Marian's boots were much more comfortable. She plucked her jacket from the hook on the wall and slid into it. She looped the strap of her purse over her shoulder and opened the door.

Jamison stood in the hallway, his fist in the air as if he were preparing to knock. They both jumped then snickered. He said, "I thought you were still here. Need a lift?"

She hesitated. Did she want to be trapped in the car with him? His face wore a look of eager expectation. Why not? She only had a few more days to enjoy his company, and he hadn't mentioned New York in a couple of days.

Turning off the light, she stepped out of the room. "Sure. It beats the tube, although they're probably not too crowded at this hour."

"Excellent."

Their footsteps tapped against the stone floors as they wove through the dimly lit building to the front doors. He pushed the door and gestured for her to go out then he shut off the lights. His car waited at the curb, purring softly. She turned and smiled as he said, "Your chariot awaits, my lady."

She giggled, and he opened the passenger car door for her. She ducked inside, and he closed it with a gentle click. He trotted to his side of the car and slid inside. Guiding the vehicle down the lane, he glanced at her for a moment before turning his attention back to the road. "Thanks for letting me take you home. I've been looking for an opportunity to speak with you."

Leighanne's pulse quickened, and her palms slicked.

Chapter Twenty-Three

Jamison's body sagged as the curtain rose and fell for the third and final time while thunderous applause filled the room. The cast and crew had taken multiple bows, and Mr. Tillinghast strutted backstage bestowing congratulations to each person. He fawned over Leighanne, one manicured hand lying on her shoulder. A polite smile rested on her face.

He mused about last night's conversation during the drive. Had she noticed his nervousness? Ever polite, she hadn't said anything about his constant drumming on the steering wheel. She hadn't seemed surprised when he told her that Tillinghast had admitted to being behind the arrow debacle. Apparently she was used to this sort of cut-throat behavior. Typical of the man, he had not apologized for his antics but rather given a ponderous soliloquy as to why he was justified in what he did. Jamison would not miss working for him.

Then the discussion turned to her new production. Her body had vibrated with excitement, and her face had been animated.

Yes, it was best that she was leaving. She would only be held back in England.

The troupe milled around props, flower bouquets and costume racks. The show could not have gone any better. Leighanne rose to the occasion and immersed herself in the part of Maid Marian. They all had, but after watching her, he could see why she was a sought-after actress on Broadway.

He glanced at his watch. Time to do a little acting of his own. He found one of the chairs from the castle scene and pushed it onto the stage. Climbing onto it, he clapped his hands several times and waited for the group to quiet down. "Words cannot express the depth of my appreciation for each one of you. The number of hours you put in learning your lines, creating props, sets and costumes, publicizing the event to your friends and family, selling tickets...the list goes on. Thanks to Leighanne for taking on the role of Maid Marian after Louise hurt herself. I can honestly say I've never seen such a flawless performance. Please give yourselves a hand."

For several moments, whistles and applause filled the platform until Jamison raised his hands again. The noise slowly abated, and he gestured to Mr. Tillinghast and Leighanne. "Our heartfelt thanks also go to Mr. Tillinghast for his generous sponsorship of our little endeavor. We could not do this without you, sir."

Clapping began again, and Mr. Tillinghast tipped his head in acknowledgment. He pointed at Leighanne and said, "We owe a debt of gratitude to Ms. Webster here, who traveled all the way from America to assist us. Granted she didn't realize she would be joining us on stage when she agreed to come, but she jumped right in when we had a need."

Tillinghast bowed to Leighanne, and her face reddened. The applause commenced again. She lifted her hand in brief acknowledgment and shrugged.

Jamison raised his voice above the commotion, "The cast party is at Kelli's place. I know it's late, but try to make an appearance if you can in order to bid farewell to Leighanne, who has a nine o'clock flight tomorrow morning. Then it will be all hands on deck Monday night to break down and pack things away for next year."

He jumped down from the chair and took a long look at Leighanne, memorizing her appearance – her smooth complexion, the riot of dark curls that framed her face. He would go to the hospital and keep Lily company rather than attend the party. Even if she was sleeping. Once her operation was over, and she had fully recovered, they would make a fresh start somewhere else. Nottingham held too many memories. He needed to make new ones. There were plenty of museums and castles scattered throughout England where he could docent.

Leighanne glanced up. Their eyes caught and held. Time stood still then Tom Haddonfield called her name, and she broke contact. She turned toward Tom, and Jamison sighed. He took one last look at her then pivoted and slipped backstage and out of the building.

Movement flashed in the corner of Leighanne's vision, and she turned to see Jamison's retreating figure. Where was he going with such purpose? He hadn't said goodbye. Would he be at the party? Would she see him before her flight to New York?

New York. Hot tears sprang to her eyes unbidden. Why did she suddenly feel like this was the worst decision of her life?

Chapter Twenty-Four

Thunderous applause deafened Leighanne as she took her bows. After three long months of rehearsals, her first performance of the New York production was behind her. God had been faithful, and her panic attacks were a thing of the past. She glanced at the cast members gathered around her, their faces bright in the glittering lights.

Dozens of audience members trotted toward the stage with bouquets. Carnations, daisies, snapdragons, yellow roses, red roses – lots of red roses. Some would include phone numbers and declarations of love. She shook her head. How could someone propose to a person they had never met?

A young woman with flowing blonde hair and tentative smile handed her an arrangement of lilies nestled in baby's breath. Leighanne dipped her head toward the white star-shaped blooms, their tangy fragrance filling her nose. One of the stage hands trotted to her and took the myriad cellophane wrapped bunches from her arms. She smiled and said, "Thank you. They were getting heavy. I'd like to keep the lilies, if you don't mind."

The lanky crew member flushed and stammered, "No problem, Ms. Webster. I'll put the rest in your dressing room." He backed away and was swallowed up in the cast who continued to mill around the stage.

Leighanne touched the yellow-green leaves and pressed her lips together as her eyes welled with tears. Kelli called to share the news that Mr. Tillinghast had come through with the money as promised, and the operation had been a total success. Jamison's sister Lily was going to be fine. She was back in her own place and had taken a part-time job at a high-end jewelry store near her flat. Thank you, Lord.

Kelli also told her about Jamison. Leighanne hoped her attempt at nonchalance sounded genuine. According to her sister, he quit his job at the museum and moved to London, where he accepted a position at The British Museum. Was he happy there? Did he think of her, or had he swept her out of his memory?

Leighanne's vision raked the auditorium, her eyes darting from face to face. Who was she searching for? She didn't have any friends outside the theatre, and Kelli and Maurice were on holiday in Brighton with the kids. It wasn't like they could jump on a plane to come see her. And Jamison...

Her head throbbed in the glare of the lights. Sweat beaded at her hairline and above her lip, but she resisted the urge to wipe at it. Otherwise, she would get a handful of makeup. The cast pressed closer as they chattered like magpies. One of the production assistants pushed her way through the crowd carrying a towel and a glass of water. Leighanne could have hugged her.

"Here you are, Ms. Webster. You look like you could use some refreshment."

Leighanne took the towel and dabbed at the moisture on her face. "Thanks, Christina. You're a peach."

The girl smiled and ducked her head. "Just doing my job."

Leighanne took in the young woman's appearance, and it was as if she was seeing the young woman for the first time. Always impeccably dressed and never with a hair out of place, Christina was efficient and gracious no matter how tense things got around the theatre. She anticipated the cast and crew's needs and seemed to be everywhere at the same time.

Christina turned, and Leighanne laid a hand on her shoulder. "And you're wonderful at it. We couldn't put on this play without you."

Christina blushed and ducked her head.

Leighanne leaned closer. "I'm serious, Christina. You're very good. Do you have goals to be a full producer at some point? I think you could do it."

The woman's eyes widened. "You think so? I do want to be a producer someday."

"You have the makings of being a great one. I'll mention this to Preston. He's well connected, you know. Perhaps he can find an opportunity for you."

Christina's voice came out as a squeak, "You'd do that for me? Why?"

Leighanne shrugged. "We look out for each other. Someone helped me when I first arrived. Now it's my turn to pay it forward. In fact, I should have done something like this a long time ago." She frowned. "Unfortunately, I was too focused on myself."

"Ms. Webster!"

Leighanne looked toward the voice, and she gaped. Mindy, another one of the production assistants, approached clutching a huge bouquet of black-eyed Susans. Bundled in a bed of feathery ferns, dozens of golden yellow blooms bobbed as the woman rushed toward her.

The assistant thrust the flowers into Leighanne's arms and said, "These just came for you. Aren't they gorgeous?" Mindy turned to Christina. "One of the costumers is looking for you."

Christina thanked Leighanne before hustling backstage.

Leighanne's breath stuttered, and she nodded as Mindy moved away. Finding her voice, Leighanne called out, "Wait! Who brought these? Where are they from?"

Mindy wheeled back and shrugged. "I'm not sure. Pete is the one who took the delivery. He was busy packing and asked me to give them to you."

"Uh...okay. Thanks." Leighanne touched one of the petaled heads with a gentle finger. If she didn't know better, she'd think they were from Jamison. He knew they were her favorite flower. But Jamison was somewhere in England. Maybe they were from Kelli. She wanted to come, but it hadn't worked out.

The rest of the cast had vacated the stage, and the crew worked around Leighanne setting up for the tomorrow's production. She needed to shed her costume and get home. A hot bath and a cup of herbal tea would help curb the adrenaline and allow her to fall asleep.

She slipped behind the curtain and walked through the maze of hallways toward her dressing room. She rounded the corner and froze. Jamison! Standing outside her room, a brown fedora gripped in his hands. His face split into a smile. "I see you got my flowers."

Leighanne stared at him, her mind in an uproar. "What? How? You're here!"

"I am. And if you'll have me, I'd like to stay."

"What are you saying?"

He gestured toward the door. "How about if we discuss this

inside?"

She slapped her forehead and hurried forward. "Of course."

He turned the knob and pushed open the door. Leighanne walked inside, hoping her trembling legs would get her across the room to the couch. She sank into the cushions, bouquet still clutched in her arms. He took them from her and laid them on the end table. Lowering himself beside her, he drew her cold hands into his.

"Jamison..."

"Leighanne..."

Jamison stroked the back of her hand with his thumb, and Leighanne's heart thudded. He smirked. "As a gentleman, I should let you go first, but I'd rather you hear me out before you say anything."

Mutely, she nodded.

He shifted closer and lifted her chin so he could meet her eyes. "I love you."

"What..."

Jamison put a finger to her lips for a moment. "Don't stop me, or I'll lose my nerve."

She folded her hands in her lap. "Okay."

"I love you. I always have. I didn't realize until I saw you again. I hurt you when I broke off our relationship. I thought I knew better than God." A rueful look swept over his face. "And we both know *that's* not true." He reached over and tucked a strand of her hair behind her ear, and she shivered at his touch. "I need you, Leighanne. I'm making a mess of this, and I don't know how to work it all out, but I want to be with you. Forever. If you'll have me, that is. Will you marry me?"

Leighanne's eyes widened. He did love her, and he wanted to marry her. He came all the way over here to tell her. Ambition warred with love. "I...I...I don't know."

His face fell, and he raked his hands through his hair before climbing to his feet. "That's it then. I guess I was a fool to think you could possibly still love me."

She grabbed his hand and yanked him back down on the sofa. "I do love you. More than anything, but is it possible to have a successful marriage? Are you asking me to return to England? I'm not ready to do that. What if you stay in the States and end up resenting my career? I don't want to do this halfway."

He pulled her into a tight hug and spoke against her neck. "You're a wonderful actress, and I know how important your career is to you. God wouldn't have given you this gift if he didn't want you to use it. I want to stay in America...with you! I'll apply for my visa and, when I'm allowed to work, will find something that compliments your schedule." He waggled his eyebrows. "Or I could stay home and be a kept man."

She gave him a playful slap on the arm then took a deep breath and closed her eyes. Could she do this? Lord, help me.

I'm here, my child. What I have drawn together, no man can break.

Warmth filled Leighanne, and she opened her eyes to find Jamison staring at her. Love shone from his eyes, and anticipation was etched on his face.

She nodded and said, "Yes."

"Yes?"

"Yes."

He fist pumped the air and whooped before pulling her into a bear hug. They clung together for several moments then he rose and drew her to her feet. Cupping her face in his hands, he whispered, "You've made me the happiest man on earth." He lowered his head, and their lips met in a gentle kiss.

Leighanne sighed and laid her head against his chest, his heart beating steadily in her ear. Thank you, Lord.

THE END

What did you think of *Love Found in Sherwood Forest?*

Thank you so much for purchasing *Love Found in Sherwood Forest*. You could have selected any number of books to read, but you chose this book.

I hope it added encouragement and exhortation to your life. If so, it would be nice if you could share this book with your family and friends by posting to Facebook (www.facebook.com) and/or Twitter (www.twitter.com).

If you enjoyed this book and found some benefit in reading it, I'd appreciate it if you could take some time to post a review on Amazon, Goodreads, Kobo, GooglePlay, Apple Books, or other book review site of your choice. Your feedback and support will help me to improve my writing craft for future projects and make this book even better.

Thank you again for your purchase.

Blessings,

Linda Shenton Matchett

Acknowledgements

Although writing a book is a solitary task, it is not a solitary journey. There have been many who have helped and encouraged me along the way.

My parents who presented me with my first writing tablet and encouraged me to capture my imagination with words. Thanks, Mom and Dad!

Scribes212 – my ACFW on-line critique group: Marcy Dyer, Valerie Goree, Marcia Lahti, Catherine Leggitt, and the late Loretta Boyett (passed on to Glory, but never forgotten). Without your input, my writing would not be nearly as effective. (Where did I put that clue?)

My Wolfeboro critique group – we never did come up with a name! Helen Fernald, Cindy Scott, and Suzanne Simmons. Your feedback and encouragement have been invaluable.

Eva Marie Everson – my mentor/instructor with Christian Writers' Guild. You took a timid, untrained student and turned her into a writer. Many thanks!

SincNE, and the folks who coordinate the Crimebake Writing Conference. I have attended many writing conferences, but without a doubt, Crimebake is one of the best.

Special thanks to Hank Phillippi Ryan, Halle Ephron, and Roberta Isleib for your encouragement and spot-on critiques of my work.

Tiger Wiseman – Thanks for providing the perfect writing get-away weekend. Your home is gorgeous, and you are the perfect hostess! Give Murphy a hug for me.

My husband Wes deserves special kudos for understanding my need to write. Thank you for creating my writing room – it's perfect, and I'm thankful for it every day. Thank you for your willingness to accept a house that's a bit cluttered, laundry that's not always done, and meals on the go. I love you.

And finally, to God be the glory. I thank Him for giving me the gift of writing and the inspiration to tell stories that shine the light on his goodness and mercy.

Read on for the first chapter in *Love's Harvest*, Book one in the Wartime Bride series; retellings of biblical stories set during WWII. *Volga Region, Russia, 1923*

Chapter One

"We'll die if we don't leave this place. Pack only what you can carry." Edmund Hirsch poked his bony arms into the sleeves of his wool coat that sported more holes than Swiss cheese. A paroxysm of coughing gripped his body, the result of a mustard gas attack on his German platoon nine years ago during The Great War.

After several minutes the coughing ceased, and he mopped the sweat from his forehead with a dingy, gray handkerchief. "Be ready. We set out tomorrow at first light."

"Where will we go, *Vati*?" Five-year-old Conrad's voice trembled.

"Don't be a baby, Conrad." Older by two minutes, Conrad's twin brother, Manfred, finished tying his boot laces and jumped off the chair, his shoes clomping against the bare wood floor. His bright blue eyes blazed above his hollow cheeks.

"Hush, children." Noreen stroked Conrad's white-blond hair and met her husband's terse look with one of her own. "You heard your father. There's no time to waste."

———————•————————

Noreen yanked the zipper closed on her over-stuffed canvas satchel. Always resourceful, Edmund had attached straps to the moss-green bag so she could wear it on her back. She would also carry a suitcase in each hand. The journey promised to be arduous.

Sighing, she wiped a weary hand across her dry eyes. Even if she had any tears remaining, crying was useless. It would not make their situation less dire.

Muted voices and the occasional bump filtered through the ceiling from the boys' bedroom above. Noreen shivered and hunched into her threadbare, ruby-red sweater. An impulse purchase made during her honeymoon, the garment held more memories than warmth. Edmund insisted it brought out the roses in her cheeks.

She tossed the bulging satchel to the floor and turned her attention to the yawning luggage on the bed. Two steel pots and a fry pan nestled in the bottom of one boxy, brown suitcase between faded blue towels that had been a belated wedding present from her mother and father.

Hopefully, Edmund would find somewhere they could live in his home country with enough food to actually cook. Here, along the Volga River in Russia, the crops had failed again, and the famine was entering its second year. The decision whether to eat or plant their seed wheat had caused many families to die of starvation.

Shuffling footsteps sounded behind her. She turned as Edmund enveloped her in his arms. Nestling against his too-thin chest, she breathed in his musky scent. He bent and kissed her forehead, his black beard scraping her skin.

"You work too hard." He tucked a stray strand of her nutmeg-colored hair behind her ear.

She leaned into his touch. "Isn't that why you married me?"

"No, *Schatzi,* it is most certainly not." He grinned. "You stole my heart. I had to marry you, or I would die a broken man."

"Don't joke about that. Our friends are dying every day." She frowned. "Who knew this famine would last so long? If it weren't for the bit of help arriving from America's Volga Relief Society, matters would be much worse."

"They are sending more assistance than we are receiving. Jakob told me there is proof the government is confiscating some of the packages and keeping the money to construct new buildings and conduct repairs. As always, development of the country is valued above the lives of the people."

"Shhh!" She pressed the work-worn fingers of her right hand against his lips. "You could get in trouble for saying that. Then where would we be?"

Edmund hugged her. "There is no one to hear us, but I understand your fear. Many unexplained disappearances make for extreme caution." He released her and gestured toward the pile of clothes on their bed. "Enough depressing talk. What can I do to help?"

"Do you have our passports? With the government ratcheting up the price, we have no more savings to purchase new ones."

"Now who's speaking out against the authorities?" He patted the breast pocket of his coat. "I have the passports and our traveling papers safe and sound."

"Good." Noreen waved him away. "Then go see what the boys are about. I gave explicit instructions about what to pack, but they have a mind of their own." She shook her head. "Well, Manfred does. Conrad simply tags along."

He kissed the tip of her nose and raised his hand in mock salute. "*Jawohl!*"

She giggled and pushed him out of the room. Closing the door behind him, she sobered and dropped to her knees next to the bed. "Dear Heavenly Father, thank You for Edmund. He is a good man. Give him strength for the journey and keep us safe as we travel. Soften the hearts of his family so they will welcome us home."

Home.

Berlin was Edmund's home. Not hers.

English born and bred, Noreen stroked the floral bedspread as visions of daffodils in Regents Park flitted through her head, their golden yellow blooms swaying in the breeze. Big Ben soaring into the sky. Tower Bridge spanning the River Thames. Pristine white swans fishing the waters of Serpentine Lake in Hyde Park where a chance meeting changed the trajectory of her life.

In an effort to heal his damaged lungs, Edmund moved to London after the war. Someone told him the damp English air would act as a balm. A lover of art, he had attended the Spring Festival where she sat under a tent selling her baskets.

She climbed to her feet, and her gaze sought out the willow basket on their dresser. The basket Edmund purchased when he returned to her booth after taking his girlfriend home. His last date with the woman.

Noreen's smile broadened. Who knew basket weaving would catch her a husband? She flushed as she remembered the conversation.

"If I purchase this basket, will you go out with me?"

"What about your girlfriend?"

"I told her we were finished, that I was going to marry you."

"Isn't that a bit rash? You don't even know me."

"I know enough."

After a whirlwind courtship, Edmund asked for her hand in marriage. Her parents objected, so Edmund took her to the register office where he wed her in front of two gray-haired, bored-looking clerks. A year later the twins were born, and her parents decided being grandparents was more important than holding a grudge. They eventually grew to love their German son-in-law as much as their daughter did. Enough to support the family's move to Russia in another effort to heal Edmund's lungs. She swallowed against the lump in her throat. Her parents' death last year in a train accident still stung.

Overheard, a thump followed by laughter broke her reverie. Warmth filled her. She loved her country, but she loved Edmund more. That is why she would leave all but her most necessary possessions and travel to yet another foreign country to live with her in-laws. People she had never met who spoke a language she didn't know.

Other Titles

Romance
Love's Harvest, Wartime Brides, Book 1
Love's Rescue, Wartime Brides, Book 2
Love's Belief, Wartime Brides, Book 3
Love's Allegiance, Wartime Brides, Book 4
On the Rails
A Love Not Forgotten (Coming March 2020)
A Doctor in the House:
(The Hope of Christmas Collection)

Mystery
Under Fire
Under Ground
Under Cover

Murder of Convenience, Women of Courage, Book 1

Non-Fiction
WWII Word Find, Volume 1

Linda Shenton Matchett writes about ordinary people who did extraordinary things in days gone by. She is a volunteer docent and archivist at the Wright Museum of WWII and a trustee for her local public library. Born in Baltimore, Maryland, a stone's throw from Fort McHenry, she has lived in historical places most of her life. Now located in central New Hampshire, Linda's favorite activities include exploring historic sites and immersing herself in the imaginary worlds created by other authors.

Website/blog: http://www.LindaShentonMatchett.com

Facebook:
http://www.facebook.com/LindaShentonMatchettAuthor

Pinterest: http://www.pinterest.com/lindasmatchett

Amazon: https://www.amazon.com/Linda-Shenton-Matchett/e/B01DNB54S0

Goodreads: http://www.goodreads.com/author_linda_matchett

Bookbub: http://www.bookbub.com/authors/linda-shenton-matchett